Bex Carter 1:

Aunt Jeanie's Revenge

Aunt Jeanie's Revenge
Book 1 of the Bex Carter

Other books by Tiffany Nicole Smith:

Fairylicious
Fairylicious Book 1

Delaney Joy, Fairy Exterminator
Fairylicious Book 2

Bex Carter, Fairy Protector
Fairylicious Book 3

D.J. McPherson, Fairy Hunter
Fairylicious Book 4

Bex Carter, Middle School Disaster
Fairylicious Book 5

The Bex Carter Series

ISBN: **978-1492952770**

Cover Design by Creative Motions

Twisted Spice Publications

To everyone who reads my stories—thank you.

I'd love to hear from you!

Twitter: @Tigerlilly79
Facebook: https://www.facebook.com/tiffany.smith.735944
Website: authortiffanynicole.com
Email: authortiffanynicole@gmail.com

Bex Carter: 1

Aunt Jeanie's Revenge

Tiffany Nicole Smith

1

Rebecca Lorraine Carter

vs.

Margaret Jean Maloney

(AKA Aunt Jeanie/ AKA Aunt Meanie)

waves hello

Hello. My name is Rebecca Lorraine Carter, but everyone calls me Bex. I'm thirteen and in the seventh grade at Lincoln Middle School. My life is okay, but it's definitely not normal. First let me give you a rundown of my not-so-normal family:

Bex: Awesome-Possum super-cool middle-schooler

Reagan (Ray): Bratty little sister extraordinaire

Priscilla: Pain in the butt #1

Penelope: Ditto #2

Francois: Ditto #3   AKA Triple Terrors!

Aunt Jeanie: My crazy nut of an aunt

Uncle Bob: The poor guy who somehow got stuck with my crazy nut of an aunt—he's very nice and very rich.

Aunt Alice: The best aunt eva! Seriously though, she's my best grown-up friend.

Nana: My heart and soul. The sweetest grandma in the world.

Dad: In prison (long story)

Mom: ???? (even longer story)

I live with my Aunt Jeanie and Uncle Bob in their humongous house with their terrible triplets and my seven-year-old sister, Reagan.

We used to live with Nana, but she started having some problems and the social worker said she wasn't equipped to take care of us anymore. I didn't agree with that at all, but I was just a kid, so of course I had no say in the matter.

It's been a few years since Ray and I had parents. My father was in prison for stealing from his job and my mother had taken off a little before that. She went on a trip to Europe with her friends and never came back. We lived with Nana for a couple of years and then we moved to the Maloney residence.

Aunt Jeanie and I had never gotten along very well, so you can imagine that I wasn't too thrilled with the transition. Don't get me wrong; I love my aunt, but most times I just don't like her. I know that seems like a terrible thing to say, but if you knew her, you would totally understand.

Aunt Jeanie is . . . well, Aunt Jeanie is a piece of work. At least that's what Nana has always said. At first I didn't understand what that meant. Whenever Nana would hang up after a phone conversation with Aunt Jeanie, she'd sigh and say, "Whew, that Jeanie is a piece of work." I know what she meant now. "Piece of work" was a classier way of saying pain in the butt. So, I have to say Aunt Jeanie is definitely a piece of work.

As far as my not liking Aunt Jeanie, she doesn't like me either. Nothing I do or say is good enough for her. Everything about me seems to offend her, especially the way I look. My thick, bushy red hair is very hard to manage. It looks like a lion's mane. Aunt Jeanie always yells at me for not taking care of it, but she doesn't understand. Her hair is short and fine. She has it easy.

I'm not super skinny and petite like she is. I'm very tall for my age and big-boned. I love to play all sorts of sports so my size is just fine with me, but Aunt Jeanie feels like I need to be on a never-ending diet.

Everything has been a constant battle between us. I actually kept score in my head. At the end of last month the scoreboard looked like this:

Bex: -5   Aunt Jeanie: 2,457,932

Since this was a new month, I thought we should start all over with a clean slate. I was learning more and more about how Aunt Jeanie's mind worked and I was sure I could beat her this time.

2

Blossoming

shudders

Aunt Jeanie thought it would be fun for us to spend our Saturday afternoon having Girl Time, just the two of us. I suggested that she have Girl Time with her own two daughters, but she told me we needed to have a "special talk." If no one has ever had a "special talk" with you, trust me; they're never good conversations. Uncle Bob was taking the rest of the kids fishing. I'd much rather have been with them.

The afternoon started off all wrong when Aunt Jeanie pulled up in front of some fancy-looking shop with a French name.

"What are we doing here?" I asked as I slid my seatbelt off.

Aunt Jeanie took the key out of the ignition. "Well, Bex, you're . . . blossoming and it's about time you wore real bras like a young lady."

I looked down at my chest. I was quite happy with the sports bras I wore. I wasn't into lace and frilly things.

"Aunt Jeanie, can't we just go to Target or something?"

"What? Absolutely not!" She was acting like I had suggested that we rummage through the garbage cans for underwear. "Come on, it'll be fun."

I sighed, opened my car door, and reluctantly followed Aunt Jeanie into the shop. Thankfully, there weren't many people inside.

"Good afternoon, Mrs. Maloney," a blond lady greeted us. "This must be Bex. I'm Marjorie." The lady held out her hand for me to shake. I shook it, wondering how she knew my name. What had Aunt Jeanie told her about me? "Follow me," the woman said, leading us to the back. "I've brought out some things for you."

She led us to a rack filled with beautiful bras in all colors. Marjorie pulled out a measuring tape. "Let me measure you just to make sure of your size."

My cheeks warmed as she wrapped the tape around my chest.

"My," Marjorie said with her eyebrows raised, "you are endowed, my dear."

"Geez, Bex," Aunt Jeanie said frowning, as if it were my fault. I didn't ask to be *endowed*.

"Okay, why don't you try these on first," Marjorie said, thrusting three bras at me. One was pink, one was black with white polka dots, and the third was purple with white flowers.

I shoved them away. "Why do I need to try on a bra? It's a bra!"

Aunt Jeanie gave me a tight smile. She always did that when she thought I was about to embarrass her. "Bex, we need to make sure they fit you properly and provide enough support."

"If they're my size, they're gonna fit."

"Bex!" Aunt Jeanie yelled and I knew she meant business.

Marjorie looked at the ground like she was embarrassed for me and I took the bras from her. I went into a dressing room and tried on just one.

"Okay, it fits," I called from the dressing room.

"Let us see," Aunt Jeanie replied.

Was she serious? That was where I had to draw the line. "You can't see me in my underwear!" The looks she gave me when I was fully dressed were bad enough.

"Sweetheart, we're all girls here," Marjorie said. "Trust me, I've seen it all."

Well, she wasn't going to see me. I put my own bra and shirt back on while Aunt Jeanie banged on the door of the dressing room. "Bex, I mean it."

I opened the door. "Sorry, I changed already."

Aunt Jeanie huffed and snatched the bras away from me. "What is your problem?" she asked through gritted teeth.

I shrugged. "It's not a big deal, Aunt Jeanie." Sheesh. Can't a girl have some level of privacy?

Aunt Jeanie smiled and handed the bras to Marjorie. "We'll take these."

While Aunt Jeanie paid for the bras, I stood at the door, knowing I would pay for my disobedience later.

After bra shopping, I expected Aunt Jeanie to take me home and not speak to me for the rest of the day, but instead she took me to a coffee shop.

She ordered some kind of latté and I ordered a hot chocolate.

"Would you like whipped cream and sprinkles?" asked the man at the counter.

"No, she will not," Aunt Jeanie answered before I could open my mouth.

"Aww, but I wanted whipped cream and sprinkles," I whined as we made our way to an empty table.

"Do you know how many calories are in just a dab of whipped cream?"

I didn't, but I figured it had a lot because it tasted so good.

I stared out the window while we waited for our orders. I didn't like being alone with Aunt Jeanie. Our conversations were always filled with awkward silences and me saying the wrong things. I'd had enough awkwardness for the day.

Aunt Jeanie took a deep breath. "Bex, since you're a teenager now, I think we should discuss, you know, the birds and the bees."

A knot formed in my stomach. "Aunt Jeanie, Nana and I already had that discussion. I know everything I need to know."

Aunt Jeanie released a sigh of relief. "Good. That's great. I'll be having that talk with the triplets soon so I could use some practice. If you have any questions about anything, please feel free to ask."

"Sure, Aunt Jeanie. I'll do that." I would absolutely *not* be doing that. She was not going to use me as some crash test dummy so she could get it right when it came to her kids.

A server brought over our drinks. Aunt Jeanie sipped hers while I blew on my hot chocolate.

"Bex, how do you feel about boys?"

I cringed. I knew this talk was coming, ever since I'd seen a book called *Talking to Today's Teen* on the coffee table with the corner folded down on a page that was titled "The Dating Scene."

I fiddled with the sugar packets. "They're okay, I guess. I have a few friends who are boys—Maverick, Jeeves, and Santiago."

"Yes, but I mean boys that are more than friends."

I wondered what Ray and the triplets were doing. I would give anything to be on a boat fishing with them and not having this embarrassing conversation. "I'm confused, Aunt Jeanie. Before, you told me I couldn't have a boyfriend before I graduated college."

She nodded. "I did say that, didn't I? I've had time to think about it and I know that's not really fair or realistic. Still, you're not going to be dating for some time. Even so, I was in junior high once. I know you must have a crush on someone. Austin maybe?"

I slid down in my seat. Austin was the son of one of Aunt Jeanie's friends. He'd taken me to my sixth-grade Valentine's Dance and we'd really hit it off. I did like Austin as more than a friend, but he wasn't my boyfriend, at least not yet. Aunt Alice was the only grown-up I talked to about Austin.

"We're just friends," I said.

Aunt Jeanie stared at me over the rim of her coffee cup. I sank even lower in my seat. At this rate I'd be drinking my hot chocolate from under the table. "Are you sure Nana told you everything?" she asked.

"Yes, Aunt Jeanie."

"It would be really irresponsible of me to not educate you properly."

"It's okay, Aunt Jeanie."

She placed her coffee cup on the table and raised one eyebrow at me. She was really good at the one-eyebrow raise. "Do you know where babies come from?"

I closed my eyes and put my palm on my forehead. "Aunt Jeanie, please. Mom and Dad told me. Nana told me. We watched the video in Ms. Warbler's class last year. I know."

For some reason this wasn't good enough for her. "See, Bex, when—"

I put my fingers in my ears. "La, la, la, la, la, la," I sang, completely aware of how foolish I looked and that people were staring. We were *not* discussing *that*.

"Bex, cut it out!" Aunt Jeanie said, looking around. "Fine, we'll discuss it another time."

No, we would discuss it never. I changed the subject by asking Aunt Jeanie what she planned on planting in the spring and she rambled on about peonies and lilies. I sat up a little straighter in my seat, proud that I had managed to save myself from that horrific conversation.

Bex: 1   **Aunt Jeanie: 0**

3

The Silver Roses

rolls eyes

When we got home, Uncle Bob and the kids were still out. That was disappointing because that meant more quality Bex-Aunt Jeanie time. I didn't think I could take any more.

I had gone upstairs to place my brand new bras in a drawer when Aunt Jeanie called me back downstairs to the living room. I prayed that it wasn't for a continuation of the talk she'd tried to have in the coffee shop.

The coffee table was littered with pictures, paint squares, and fabric swatches.

"What's all this?" I asked.

Aunt Jeanie patted the area next to her on the sofa. "Come have a seat. I want to show you something."

I sat beside her with my guard up. I never knew what to expect from her.

She held up a lime green paint square. "Since green and yellow are your favorite colors, I thought this would go nicely on the walls and then we could incorporate some green and yellow accessories."

"Aunt Jeanie, what are you talking about?"

"Changing the guestroom into your bedroom."

My eyes widened. I had been asking her to do this for months. A thirteen-year-old having to share a room with a seven-year-old, especially a seven-year-old like Reagan, was just unacceptable. I needed my privacy.

"Look at this bed," Aunt Jeanie said, handing me a picture.

It was one of the coolest beds I'd ever seen. I would have to climb a tiny staircase to get to the top to sleep and underneath it was a desk. I took a look at the other pictures spread before me. Sphere lanterns, oddly-shaped rugs, curtains, wall decals—I had to have this room. I couldn't believe Aunt Jeanie was actually giving it to me after all this time.

"So, what do you think?" Aunt Jeanie asked.

"I absolutely love it. All of it."

"Good," Aunt Jeanie said. "This can all be yours . . . on one condition."

Of course there was a condition. "What's that?"

She pulled a brochure from behind the sofa pillow. "You have to become a Silver Rose."

"A what?"

"A Silver Rose."

I took the brochure from her. "You mean those snobby rich girls who dress up in ball gowns and act like they're better than everyone else?"

"No! I mean those enlightened girls who do community service and set an example for the youth of our town. The Silver Rose Society is for girls ages sixteen through eighteen and the Junior Silver Roses are girls thirteen through fifteen. This would be a great experience for you."

I placed the brochure on the sofa. "Aunt Jeanie, have we never met? You know very well that this kind of stuff isn't for me. I'm more of a soccer-playing, movie-watching kind of girl."

"Oh, that's too bad. I would have had a lot of fun decorating this bedroom for you."

I thought about that for a moment. I totally needed my own space. I couldn't even have friends over without Ray being annoyingly disruptive. The room looked like the rooms I'd seen on TV and I wanted it. I figured an absolutely cool bedroom would last longer than the process of becoming a member of that stupid group. I didn't feel one hundred percent about it, but I accepted Aunt Jeanie's offer and we shook on it. Aunt Jeanie had found a way to get me to do something she wanted me to do, so I guess this round goes to her.

Bex: 1　　　　　**Aunt Jeanie: 1**

4

Girl World

—feeling confused ☹

<u>Junior Silver Rose Candidate Response Journal Page 2</u>

1. Why do you want to join this prestigious organization?

I don't, but I really want my own super-cool room.

2. What are you hoping to gain from this experience?

A new room.

3. What do you like most about this organization?

????? You should really be asking my Aunt Jeanie this question.

4. What will you add to this organization should you be accepted as a member?

See no. 3

5. What is something you need to work on?

See no. 3

6. Why do you think you will be a great fit for us?

I don't.

7. Which of our founders do you look up to the most?

Really, my aunt should be filling this out.

"Dagnabbit, Bex, this sounds like the most horrible thing ever," my friend Chirpy said during lunch on Monday. "You have to get out of this."

"I can't," I told her. "You should have seen the pictures she showed me. I have to have that room."

Lily-Rose took the brochure from Chirpy. "This sounds like something my parents would make me do." She was right. Lily-Rose's parents were tight and strict like Aunt Jeanie.

"Bex, zat sounds like a nightmare," Marishca stated in her Russian accent that I loved. "I'm so sorry."

Marishca, Lily-Rose, and Chirpy were the best friends I'd ever had. We'd gone through some rough times recently, but now we were doing pretty well.

Lily-Rose, Chirpy, and I met in the first grade. They were small for their age and I was big for my age. I kind of acted as their bodyguard when they were getting picked on, and we've been stuck together ever since.

Marishca moved here from Russia a few years ago and became the fourth member of our tribe. When we were together I looked totally out of place. They were all short and skinny, while I was really tall and not skinny. Lily-Rose Johnston had brown skin with dark hair and large pink glasses. Chirpy got her name back in the first grade because we thought she had a big nose that looked like a bird's beak and the name had stuck. Her real name was Beatrice Martin. Chirpy and Marishca Baranov both had short hair and brown eyes, although Chirpy's hair was light brown and Marishca's was blond.

I squeezed hot sauce on my taco. "Lily-Rose, maybe I should ask Aunt Jeanie to tell your parents about the Silver Roses and we can do it together."

Lily-Rose's eyes widened. "Don't you dare! Bex, I'd never speak to you again."

I shrugged. At least once a month my friends gave me the silent treatment for doing something stupid, so that really wasn't a big deal to me. I couldn't blame them though; I did have a knack for causing trouble.

"I hate to be a wet rag, but what if you don't make it?" Chirpy asked. (Please excuse my friend. You'll get used to her old-people lingo.)

"No new room for me," I replied. Not making it was a very real possibility. I had stayed up all night reading the brochure about the four pillars of being an empowered woman: selflessness, business knowledge, etiquette, and physical appearance. Then to add insult to injury, Aunt Jeanie had handed me a booklet called a response journal filled with questions I had to answer throughout the process, as if I didn't have enough homework already.

Marishca flipped through my response journal. "I can tell you one zing. You're not going to make it based on zese answers."

"What? They said to be honest," I replied.

"Look," Chirpy said, nodding toward something behind me.

I turned to see the Avas—Ava G., Ava T., and Ava M.—sitting alone at a table. That was a rare occurrence. Ava G., the worst of the Avas, had been the most popular girl in the seventh grade, but then she was caught talking trash about kids who were supposed to be her friends and they deserted her. When I say caught, I mean I recorded her and somehow it got played over the school intercom, but that's a whole other story.

Now Kristen Lee was the most popular girl and she and Ava were involved in this huge ongoing fight. My friends and I stayed out of it. We had each other and we couldn't care less about being popular. I'd rather have three real friends than a hundred fake ones. A while ago my friends had thought that it was very important for us to be popular this school year, but I showed them the error of their ways and now they were acting normal again. Well, almost normal.

Speaking of Kristen Lee . . .

"Hey, guys," she said, taking a seat at our table next to Lily-Rose.

"Hey," we muttered, exchanging glances. What was she doing sitting with us?

"Bex, can I talk to you for a minute?" she asked.

"Sure," I answered, taking a bite of my taco. I quickly grabbed my bottle of water. I'd put too much hot sauce on it. "What's up?" I asked, after I was done coughing.

Kristen flicked her dark hair over one shoulder. "You're friends with Ava G., right?"

The G in Ava G. stood for Groves and we were so far away from being friends it wasn't even funny. Our relationship was hard to describe. Aunt Jeanie and Mrs. Groves were best friends. Aunt Jeanie made me hang out with Ava, hoping that her charm and poise would rub off on me. Really deep down inside, I think Aunt Jeanie thinks I'm a loser. Ava resented me because of this, and our time together was never pleasant. I didn't like Ava either. Sometimes she was just plain evil.

I found it strange that one, Kristen was even talking to me and two, she was asking me about her rival. "I wouldn't exactly say we were friends, but we hang out sometimes because we have to. Why?"

Kristen glared in Ava's direction. "I need you to give me the four-one-one. I heard she's been talking about me and I think she's planning something."

"Like what?" Lily-Rose asked.

"Some kind of rebellion against me," Kristen answered.

Good grief. You'd think she was the leader of a country or something. If being popular includes being sneaky and paranoid all the time, count me out.

"What does that have to do with me?" I asked. I wanted nothing to do with their stupid fight.

"I'd like you to give me a heads-up if you hear anything. There's a seat for you at my lunch table if you do."

She looked at me like I was a dog she was offering a bone to and I was just supposed to jump at the chance to be her lackey. I had never thought Kristen was as bad as Ava, but she just might be.

"No, thanks. I'm good at this table. The Awesome-Possum table is the place for me," I said proudly.

I should explain to you that the seventh-grade area of our school's cafeteria is divided into three sections; Coolville, the So-sos, and Loserville. A few months ago I had been banished to Loserville, but I wasn't a loser, so I created a section for me, my friends, and anyone else who wanted to sit there called the Awesome-Possum table.

Kristen raised her eyebrows. "Okay," she said as she got up to leave. I knew she wasn't used to getting rejected. Clearly, Kristen was winning this meaningless popularity contest, so why couldn't she just leave it at that?

In Girl World someone always had to be planning something or spreading rumors about her rival. If she didn't like someone, why not just stay away from her?

"Anyway," I said to my friends after Kristen left, "the worst part of my weekend was when Aunt Jeanie attempted to have The Talk with me." My friends groaned.

"Having The Talk with grown-ups is the worst thing ever," Lily-Rose said. "My parents actually made a PowerPoint so they wouldn't have to talk about it. They made me read the slides out loud."

Chirpy nodded. "Whenever my mom brings it up I sing a song in my head and block her out. My dad never talks about it."

"Talks about what?" Jeeves asked as he, Maverick, and Santiago took a seat at our table. Maverick gave Lily-Rose a kiss on her cheek and I tried not to roll my eyes. I wished a lunch monitor had seen that and arrested them! Well, maybe not arrested them, but they could get a detention for PDA. Principal Radcliff hated public displays of affection. They were so into each other that everyone called them MavRose. I didn't like my friend being in love, but it was something I just had to deal with.

"Nothing, Jeeves," I replied. We definitely weren't going to talk about *that* with the boys.

Jeeves was really Walter, but we called him Jeeves because he always wore a tuxedo—all day, every day.

"We were just talking about zis stupid group Bex's aunt is making her join," Marishca said.

Santiago picked up the brochure and thumbed through it. "This might be good for you, Bex. You can learn how to be a lady."

"What does that mean?" I demanded.

Santiago slowly laid the brochure back on the table. "Nothing. You're cool and everything, but you're a little rough around the edges. Like one of the guys."

I took some lettuce from my taco and threw it at him. "So, what? I'm some kind of uncivilized monkey?"

"N-no," Santiago answered. "I'm just saying—"

"He's not saying anything," Maverick said, briefly taking his attention off Lily-Rose. "Santiago, just shut up, man."

"All right," he said, digging into his food.

I didn't care what Santiago said. I was a perfect lady—when I wanted to be.

That evening Aunt Jeanie called me to the living room after dinner.

"Tomorrow is the first meeting for the Junior Silver Roses," she informed me.

I already knew that. Every Tuesday and Thursday for the next six weeks, I would have to go to boring meetings about joining this boring group.

"Now, Bex, I want you to be prepared. These girls aren't the kind you're used to hanging out with. They go to private schools and country clubs and they're very, very cultured."

Every sentence she spoke made this idea sound worse and worse. "Okay," was the only response I could muster up.

Aunt Jeanie pushed her hair behind her ears. "Of course, you must be dressed appropriately. First impressions are so important. I don't want you sticking out like a sore thumb."

In other words, don't embarrass her.

"The panel will be watching you from the second you step into the room, trying to determine if you're Silver Rose material. Everything you say and do will make a difference."

Just what I needed: more people judging me.

"Aunt Jeanie, I get it. I won't do anything wrong. I won't open my mouth. I won't even breathe."

Aunt Jeanie smiled. "Good. Mrs. Groves is bringing Ava by after school tomorrow and we'll ride to the country club together."

"What—wait. Ava is doing this too?"

"Of course. Anyone who's anyone is pledging to become a member."

If I had known this before, I probably wouldn't have accepted this offer. A new room wasn't worth having to put up with Ava G. any more than I already did.

"Aunt Jeanie, I—"

"Uh, uh, uh," Aunt Jeanie said, wagging her finger at me. "I've already paid the nonrefundable fees so there's no backing out now."

There was nothing left to say. I left the sofa and trudged up the stairs, wondering what I had gotten myself into.

Bex: 1   **Aunt Jeanie: 2**

5

First Impressions and Geraldine Cordelia Ulysses

sighs

<u>Junior Silver Rose Candidate Response Journal Page 4</u>
How do you feel about your first meeting with the Silver Roses?

I think this is a very, very, very, very extremely bad idea.

Aunt Jeanie, Mrs. Groves, Ava, and I pulled into valet parking of the Gulliver Country Club fifteen minutes before the meeting began.

I dragged behind the three of them as we entered the building. A beautiful fountain stood in the lobby. The soothing sound of the running water was drowned out by the squawking noise from the groups of women standing around talking. Aunt Jeanie spotted one of her friends as we entered the club. "Hi, Holly!"

Holly, a woman with long blond hair, waved my aunt and Mrs. Groves over.

Mrs. Groves turned to Ava and me. "Girls, you go ahead to Conference Room D. Ava, introduce Bex to the girls you know."

Ava rolled her eyes at her mother and walked away. I followed her because I had no idea where Conference Room D was.

We reached the doorway of the conference room. Inside girls wearing beautiful dresses milled around the room chatting with each other. I gulped. I hated situations like this. It seemed like everyone already knew each other.

Ava pointed her finger in my face and narrowed her green eyes at me. "Listen, you don't know me and I don't know you. Don't even look at me." Then she flicked her long, black hair over her shoulder and left me standing in the hallway.

As soon as she entered the room, a group of girls flocked around her. I swear, she was like a popularity magnet. They squealed and gave each other double air kisses.

I took a deep breath and entered the large room filled with rows of chairs. A podium stood at the front of the room. Next to the podium was a table with a stack of books.

Of course, no one paid me any attention. I looked down at the long-sleeved blue dress I wore. I had fought with Aunt Jeanie about putting it on, but I was glad she had made me wear it or I might have really looked out of place.

All the girls were engaged in conversation except for one girl sitting alone in a chair playing a game on her phone. I took the seat to her left.

For a moment she continued to play her game, not even acknowledging me, which I found extremely rude. I cleared my throat. "Hi, I'm Bex," I said, offering the girl my hand.

Finally she paused the game and shook my hand. "Geraldine Cordelia Ulysses. But you can call me Geraldine." Sheesh. I thought my name was bad.

"Nice to meet you, Geraldine. Why aren't you talking to the other girls?" She certainly didn't look like the other girls, pretty and perfectly polished.

Geraldine had long mousy brown hair that fell to her waist, pale, pale skin, and purple braces which I thought were pretty cool. She was wearing some kind of weird vest with cats on it. I didn't think that was cool.

Geraldine looked around the room. "These girls all know each other. They go to the same dance classes, the same gymnastics, the same schools; they hang out here at the country club. I don't do any of those things and I'm homeschooled."

"Oh." Geraldine didn't seem like the kind of girl who'd like to pledge to this sort of thing. "If you don't mind my asking, why are you doing this?"

Geraldine shrugged. "It's my mom's idea. Someone on the council suggested to her that if she wanted to be important, I needed to be a Silver Rose. My mom is all about making friends in high society." Her mother sounded like Aunt Jeanie.

The adults entered the room, meaning the meeting was about to begin. This was the only meeting where the parents would attend since it was the orientation. After that, it would just be the pledges.

Aunt Jeanie came up behind me. "Bex, why don't you sit closer to the front?" It sounded like a question, but the tone of her voice told me that it wasn't.

I stood and told Geraldine good-bye. Aunt Jeanie pushed me toward the front of the room. "What are you doing sitting with her? I told you first impressions are everything." She was practically pinching my arm.

"Well, where am I supposed to sit?" I asked.

"By somebody better. Look, there's Ava." It was just my luck that there was an empty seat next to her. She glared at me as I sat down like I had a flesh-eating disease or something.

A woman stood behind the podium and banged a gavel. The room became silent immediately. "Good afternoon, ladies."

"Good afternoon, Mrs. Armstrong," everyone answered in unison except for me.

"For those of you who don't know me, my name is Amelia Armstrong. I am the president of the Silver Rose Society. I have been looking forward to this year's pledge period. I heard that we have the cream of the crop pledging this year."

Every March was pledge time, according to the brochure. I would be pledging the junior chapter for girls ages thirteen through fifteen. There was another chapter for girls ages sixteen through eighteen. I hoped I wouldn't have to pledge that one also.

While Mrs. Armstrong talked about the four pillars of womanhood, I checked her out. She looked rich. I was intrigued by her hair; it was silver, not white, but silver. Her navy blue dress suit was impeccable and a delicate string of pearls dangled from her neck. I couldn't tell whether or not I would like her. Probably not.

"Tonight is our initial meet-and-greet. We will move into the other room where you may eat and mingle." Great. That meant the other girls would be mingling. I'd be standing around awkwardly.

She went over the point system. Pledges would be scored on each lesson. We would have to earn 100 out of 125 points to be accepted into the group.

Mrs. Armstrong continued. "Our first official class will be on Thursday where we will discuss physical presentation." She said some more things to the parents about us being on time and not missing any classes and then dismissed us to the other room.

I entered the meet-and-greet room and stayed as far away from Ava as possible. Tables with all sorts of fancy finger foods lined the walls. I spotted a chocolate fountain surrounded by fruits for dipping and an ice sculpture of a woman holding a bouquet of roses over her head.

I grabbed a plate and put a couple of potato wedges on it, when I realized no one else was eating. Some people walked around with cups of punch or water, but that was it. I looked around for Aunt Jeanie. She stood on the other side of the room talking to one of her tennis buddies. Our eyes met. I put the plate down on the table and she nodded. Then she waved her hand, motioning for me to get myself into the mix.

I looked around. Girls huddled in small groups, deep in conversation. What was I supposed to do? Just bust in and say, "Hey, I'm Bex. Please include me so I don't feel like a loser."

I thought about my dream room. I thought about Aunt Jeanie telling me that the selection panel would be watching my every move. I knew getting along with the other girls would be part of our final evaluation.

I approached a group of five girls.

"I can't wait. We're going there for Spring Break," said a girl with brown curly hair.

"You're going to love it, especially at nighttime. It's magical," said another girl.

"What's magical?" I asked.

They all stared at me. Their eyes scanned me from my wild frizzy hair to my two-inch silver heels. I hated when people did that. What were they thinking?

One girl gave me a little smile. "We're talking about Paris. Been there?"

A small voice inside of me told me to lie. It would be a good way to work myself into the conversation, but I pushed it away. "No. But I'd love to go there one day."

The girls nodded and gave me phony smiles. "That's nice," said a blond girl. "Anyway, the shopping is the best. You have to go to this boutique called—"

They hadn't even asked me my name or introduced themselves. I considered myself dismissed and walked away. At least I tried.

I found Geraldine standing by the ice sculpture. Maybe she wasn't like the other girls, but at least she had given me the time of day.

"Hey, Geraldine. What are you doing?"

"Just checking this baby out," she answered. "How do you think they make these things?"

I shrugged. "I'm not sure. It looks hard though."

She touched it with her finger. "Should I lick it and see if my tongue sticks to it?"

I laughed. "Yeah, Geraldine, you should totally lick it. Let's get something to eat." I was tired of trying to act cute. I was hungry and all this great food was going to waste. I had begun to walk toward the chocolate fountain when I heard a moan behind me. I turned to see Geraldine with her tongue stuck to the ice sculpture, right on the lady's armpit.

It was not a pretty sight. I tried to edge away and pretend like I didn't see it, but it was too late.

I heard someone gasp. "What on earth?"

A woman ran over to Geraldine and began scolding her. I assumed she was her mother.

"Oh, dear," said Mrs. Armstrong. "Will someone bring a cup of warm water?"

Everyone stopped talking and gathered around to watch the fool who had her tongue stuck to the ice sculpture. Part of me felt sorry for Geraldine, but the other part of me thought she shouldn't have done something so ridiculous in the first place.

Someone brought the warm water and Geraldine's mother poured it over her daughter's tongue. Thankfully that did the trick and Geraldine was separated from the ice sculpture.

"What on earth would possess you to do that?" her mother demanded.

Geraldine was still trying to get the feeling back in her tongue. She pointed at me. "Ex, he old ee oo oo it." Translated: "Bex, she told me to do it."

Everyone looked at me. "I did not! It was her idea. I just repeated it and I was totally joking."

Mrs. Ulysses looked at me accusingly. "Geraldine doesn't have much social experience. She can't really tell when people are joking and when they're not."

"How was I supposed to know that? This is not my fault," I insisted. Aunt Jeanie shook her head and looked up at the ceiling.

"Okay, ladies," said Mrs. Armstrong. "Let's carry on."

Everyone walked away either mumbling or giggling. Geraldine came over to me. "I tested the theory. My tongue got stuck."

I walked away from her and waited in the bathroom until it was time to go. First Impression = Big Gigantic Fail.

The ride home was quiet at first. Aunt Jeanie and Mrs. Groves were up front, whispering to each other. Ava was texting and ignoring all of us.

"So, did you make any friends, Bex?" Mrs. Groves asked.

Geraldine would have been my answer if she hadn't done something stupid and gotten me in trouble. I answered yes anyway because I didn't want to seem like a total loser.

"Really?" I don't know why she sounded so surprised. "Who?"

"Geraldine Ulysses," I muttered.

I saw Mrs. Groves frown from the side of her face. "Who?"

Aunt Jeanie shook her head and looked at Mrs. Groves. "You remember Carol Ulysses? Her daughter. Nobody."

Geraldine might have done something stupid, but she wasn't nobody.

"Oh, Bex. You don't want to make connections like that. You are the company you keep," Mrs. Groves said.

I hoped that wasn't true because I didn't want to be anything like the company I was keeping that very moment.

I knew I was going to hate every single moment of this Silver Rose nonsense and I'd figured out why I was in this predicament. Aunt Jeanie was paying me back for all the trouble I'd caused her and all the times I'd disappointed and embarrassed her. Probably for how I'd acted in the bra shop. This was her ultimate revenge. My aunt was a diabolical genius.

When we arrived home, Mrs. Groves and Ava headed for their car in the driveway.

"I told you to help her," Mrs. Groves said to Ava.

"I can't help her. She's hopeless," Ava replied.

I went to my room to answer the question Mrs. Armstrong had told us to answer when we got home from the meet-and-greet.

How do you feel after your first meeting with the Silver Rose Society?

I *know* this is a very, very, very terribly bad idea.

6

Snob Training 101

facepalm

<u>Junior Silver Rose Candidate Response Journal Page 8</u>
Describe your beauty regimen:

I wash my face in the morning. I wash my face at night. I brush my hair the best I can. Sometimes I wear lip gloss. Is that what you mean?

What is your best feature and why?

My size. I used to not like it because I was the biggest kid in school, but now that I'm in middle school, I'm not the biggest kid anymore. My size really comes in handy when I play basketball and soccer. People say I look older than I am. I kind of like that.

Name something about your physical appearance you may need to work on?

I'm not sure how to say this the right way, but my chest area I wish it wasn't growing so much. But there's not really anything I can do about that, right? I think the rest of me is okay.

Thursday's meeting was about our outward appearance and having pride in the way we presented ourselves to the world. Aunt Jeanie had dropped me off with a stern warning not to embarrass her any further. A woman named Ms. Polly was teaching the class. She looked to be in her twenties and appeared to think she was cuter than she was. She spent most of the evening whipping her blond extensions around.

There were twenty-one girls pledging this year and of course, I had to attract the one weirdo in the room. When I first arrived, I had taken a seat in the back row. I just wanted to be ignored and left alone. Tuesday's ice-sculpture incident was still fresh on everyone's mind.

46

Of course Geraldine found it fit to sit right smack next to me. She wore a vest like the one she had worn the other day, but this one had cupcakes instead of cats.

"Thanks a lot for the other night," I told her.

"What do you mean?"

"Seriously? You licked an ice sculpture like an idiot and then blamed it on me."

Geraldine frowned and mumbled to herself like she was trying to remember. "I said, 'Should I lick it and see if my tongue sticks to it?' and you said 'Yeah, Geraldine, you should totally lick it.' You told me to do it."

"Yeah, I said that, but I didn't mean do it. I meant don't do it because that would be incredibly stupid. I was being sarcastic."

"But you didn't say that," Geraldine said.

"Nobody says, 'I'm being sarcastic.' You just be sarcastic."

She folded her arms across her chest. "Well, how was I supposed to know that? I can't read your mind. I'm sorry I blamed you then."

I took a deep breath and decided to let it go. She obviously didn't know any better. "It's cool, Geraldine. Forget about it."

Ms. Polly took the podium and I decided within a minute that I didn't like her at all. "Girls, I'm just going to level with you," she said. "Looks are everything."

Most of the girls nodded in agreement. I looked at Geraldine and she shrugged.

"People like to say it's the inside that counts, but let me tell you, that's hogwash. Good looks can get you almost anything in this life. Your appearance is the first thing that people see and that will either attract them to you or turn them away."

Ms. Polly blabbed on about a daily skin care regimen and a proper diet.

I mostly daydreamed until she said, "What I want to do now is an initial assessment to see what we really need to work on."

She had us stand in a line facing her so she could critique our appearance. I felt like a show pony waiting for my turn in the ring.

"Very nice," she said after most of the girls she passed. Then she got to me. I held my breath. "Hold out your hands please." I held them out. Was she going to smack my hands to punish me for not being perfect enough? "Not bad, but you must stop biting your nails. I'd get some acrylics for now if I were you." Okay, that wasn't too bad. I was a nail biter and Aunt Jeanie had often told me that I needed to stop.

Next Ms. Polly went to poor Geraldine. She looked at Geraldine like she was a stinky piece of rotten cheese. Ms. Polly gently grabbed a clump of Geraldine's hair and then dropped it. "Don't worry, sweetie. We'll do the best we can."

Ms. Polly then revealed a long table filled with make-up stations and vanity mirrors. "Now we're going to practice the correct way to apply make-up. A little bit goes a long way. Too much can make you look cheap, and we don't want that. Okay, grab a make-up partner."

Before I could even think, Geraldine had dug her nails into my arm and was pulling me toward the make-up table. "Bex, I'll do you first."

"Now," Ms. Polly instructed, "you first need to determine whether your partner is a summer, fall, spring, or winter."

Geraldine quickly grabbed a container of dark green eye shadow. "This is definitely your color."

"Why?"

Geraldine rolled her eyes. "Because you're wearing a dark green dress, silly."

I hadn't paid attention to most of the class, but I distinctly remembered Ms. Polly saying never to match your eye shadow to your make-up. "Are you sure?" I asked, but she was already dabbing globs of the stuff on my eyelids and poking my eyeball in the process.

She snapped the eye shadow container shut. "That looks great."

"Let me see," I said, reaching for the mirror.

Geraldine pulled the mirror away from me. "Uh, uh, uh. Not until I'm done. The artist never reveals her masterpiece before completion." She started to apply blush to my cheeks.

"Geraldine, what's up with all those . . . unique vests you wear?"

"Oh, I make them myself."

I figured as much.

"Would you like me to make you one?" she asked.

"No! I mean, no. I wouldn't want you to go through all that trouble."

"But I'd love to do it."

"That's okay, really."

By the time Geraldine finished my make-up I looked like a rainbow had thrown up on a circus clown that exploded after eating a million jelly beans. My eyes were circled entirely by green eye shadow. Geraldine had applied gold lipstick. It looked so bad I wanted to know why they made gold lipstick to begin with. I couldn't imagine it looking good on anyone. My cheeks were purple and she'd actually applied the blush in a heart shape. To say I looked ridiculous was an understatement.

I looked around. The other girls' make-up was done perfectly. We were supposed to switch and do our partners, but we had run out of time. Geraldine was lucky. I would have definitely paid her back for what she'd done to my face. Ms. Polly told us to clean up the tables.

"Listen," a girl named Amber whispered in my ear as I threw the make-up applicators in the trashcan, "if you want any chance of making this group, you'd better ditch that loser. She tried out last year too and didn't even come close to making it."

I turned back and looked at Geraldine. She smiled and blew me a kiss. I tried to like Geraldine. She was nice, but she was quickly becoming annoying. I wasn't becoming a snob too, was I?

Aunt Jeanie looked stunned as I climbed into the car after practice. "Wow, Bex. I thought I taught you better than that."

"I didn't do this. My partner did."

Aunt Jeanie pressed her lips together and her cheeks puffed. Then she burst out into hysterical laughter.

My aunt didn't laugh a lot and I'd never seen her crack up like that. I mean she was having a real gut-buster. Not cool.

"Bex, I'm sorry," she said. She had laughed so hard tears were streaming down her face. "Let me take a picture to send to your Aunt Alice."

"No way!"

"All right, all right," she said as we pulled out of the parking lot. I thought the laughing would stop after a minute, but she laughed all the way home.

In the bathroom mirror I checked myself out again. I could see way Aunt Jeanie had laughed so hard. I even had a chuckle at my own expense.

Bex: 1   **Aunt Jeanie: 3**

7

Giving Back

headdesk

<u>Junior Silver Rose Candidate Response Journal Page 11</u>
Please submit your proposal for a community service
project. Tell us how it will benefit the community.
Describe what you would like to do on the lines below
and submit it to a panel member for approval.
I would like to hold a city-wide red velvet cupcake baking
contest. People will submit their cupcakes to me and I will
decide on the best one. This will benefit the community
because everyone will know who to go to for the best red
velvet cupcakes!   —Denied

Amelia Armstrong

The following day it was my turn to host a sleepover for my friends at Aunt Jeanie's. We used to have sleepovers every week until recently. My friends were getting older and they wanted to do other things on Friday nights. That made me a little sad, but I'd take what I could get.

"So, is it as bad as you thought it was going to be?" Lily-Rose asked from where she lounged on the bed.

"It's worse," I answered. "I don't belong in this group at all and now I have to come up with a community service project."

Chirpy looked up from painting her toenails. "What are you going to do?"

I lifted the lid of my laptop to do an Internet search on community service projects, the easier the better. "I don't know. This one girl named Geraldine wants to do something together, but I don't know if that's a great idea. She might be an even bigger disaster than me."

Lily-Rose sat up on the bed. "Wait a minute. You're not talking about Geraldine Ulysses, are you?"

"Yeah," I answered. "How do you know her?"

"We have the same violin teacher. Bex, trust me. The girl is a walking bad luck magnet and if you let her get attached to you she'll hold on like a leech until she sucks all the blood from you!"

I rolled my eyes. "Lily-Rose, that's a bit dramatic, don't you think?"

She shook her head. "Nope. Go ahead and become friends with her and see what happens if you think I'm exaggerating."

I thought about what Amber had said to me at our last class. My gut feeling had also told me to stay away from this girl, but I didn't want to be mean.

Lily-Rose left the bed and put her hand on my shoulder. "Trust me, kid. Being friends with Geraldine is the equivalent of wearing a sandwich board that reads 'I'm a loser. Throw stuff at my head.' Hey, let's make ice cream sundaes!"

"Yeah," Marishca and Chirpy agreed as the three of them ran down to the kitchen.

I followed slowly, wondering if and how I could break ties with Geraldine.

The next morning my friends left early to attend their Saturday morning classes. Marishca had gymnastics, Chirpy swimming, and Lily-Rose had violin lessons.

I planned to spend the day vegging out and watching some good action movies when Aunt Jeanie had to ruin my plans as usual.

Just when I had gotten comfortable in my beanbag chair with a bag of Twizzlers, she burst into the bedroom without even knocking.

"Aunt Jeanie, I'd appreciate it if you would at least knock," I told her as sweetly as possible.

"Bex, this is my house. When you get your own house and pay the mortgage, you can make the rules."

I sighed and focused on the television, hoping she would go away, but she wouldn't.

"So, have you decided on a service project?"

"Yes, but Mrs. Armstrong denied it," I answered. I thought my cupcake idea was great. Cupcakes make people happy and wasn't that the point?

"Good. This afternoon some of the girls are going down to the soup kitchen to make bagged lunches for the women and children's shelter. Be ready in a little bit."

I loved the way she asked whether or not I'd actually like to do it. "All right."

Two hours later we were at the soup kitchen. Aunt Jeanie had made me wear a dress even though I would be fixing food in a kitchen, which I thought was ridiculous. What was even more ridiculous was that the other girls were more dressed up than I was.

There were about ten girls there and Ava G. was one of them. A woman named Carol gave us gloves, hair nets, and a quick run-down of what we were supposed to do. I was put on the sandwich station, which I thought was the hardest job. The other girls only had to throw apples, bananas, and juice boxes into the white paper bags.

After Carol left, a girl named Tanya groaned. "I think making us wear these horrible hairnets should be punishment enough. How long do we have to stay here?"

"This isn't a punishment," I told her. "We're helping people less fortunate."

"Shut up, Bex!" Ava screamed from across the room. Anything I said seemed to annoy her. "How about you don't talk for the rest of the day?"

I sighed and turned back to my assigned job. I worked with Amber, who turned out to be pretty nice. I put ham and cheese between two slices of bread and then passed them to Amber. Amber then wrapped the sandwiches in wax paper and placed them in the paper bags.

We had done about ten sandwiches when Geraldine burst through the kitchen doors. "Hey, everyone. Sorry I'm late, but my cat threw up and I stepped in it."

Everyone moaned.

"Who invited her?" Ava asked loudly.

57

Geraldine didn't seem to take the hint that she wasn't wanted. "My mom overheard some of your mothers talking about it, so here I am."

I focused on making sandwiches and tried not to make eye contact with her. I did notice that she was wearing a vest with caterpillars on it.

Of course Geraldine made her way straight to me. "Hey, Bex, I guess I can help you make the sandwiches. I'm the best sandwich maker I know. Ask my mom."

I didn't get how she could be the best sandwich maker. Making a sandwich was just slapping things together. "That's okay, Geraldine. I have it under control."

"Why don't you help Ava with the juice boxes?" I asked.

"No way!" Ava shouted. "She knows she's not allowed anywhere near me."

"Don't even think about coming over here," another girl said.

Geraldine stood in the middle of the kitchen; I think the fact that no one wanted her there was starting to settle in. I felt awful. "Geraldine, you can put the mustard and mayonnaise packets in the bags."

Her face brightened. "Yay! I love mayo!"

Everything went fine for about fifteen minutes until some of the girls decided they had done enough work. Ava leaned against the wall and texted on her phone. A girl named Summer sat on the counter eating an apple that was meant for the lunch bags. The others, except for Amber and Geraldine, stood around talking.

"Hey," I told them, "we're not done. We have like a hundred more lunches to make."

"So make them," one girl said nastily. "I've done my time."

"What, twenty minutes? That's not fair," I told her. "You guys aren't going to get credit for this if you don't help. I'll tell Mrs. Armstrong."

A girl with shoulder-length brown hair and wearing a headband stepped up to me. "Ava, isn't this your friend?"

Ava snorted. "No."

The girl glared at me. I could see from the nameplate on her necklace that her name was Hannah. "Listen, Beck—"

"It's Bex," I corrected her. Seriously, Beck just sounds stupid.

"Whatever. You don't run anything around here so make your little lunches and shut up," Hannah said.

"Hey, don't talk to my friend like that," Geraldine said.

Hannah laughed. "Friend?"

I appreciated Geraldine trying to stick up for me, but she was only going to make things worse. "Yes, Bex is my best friend and you'd better leave her alone." Best friend? Where did that come from?

Now all the girls were laughing. "Best friend?" Ava asked, looking up from her phone. "Really, Bex. Your stupid tribe is already bad enough. This is definitely a downgrade."

"She's not my best friend," I said. The look on Geraldine's face made me feel guilty, but I was telling the truth. We weren't best friends.

"Ouch," Summer said. "Rejected."

Geraldine said nothing and continued to fill the bags with condiments.

"Hey, Geraldine," Ava said slyly, "How about adding some ketchup to the bags?"

I thought it was an odd question but for some reason Geraldine turned super pale. "Nothing in these bags needs ketchup," she said quickly.

The other girls began to mumble and giggle amongst themselves. Apparently they knew something I didn't. A girl with long black hair like Ava's went into the fridge and pulled out a bottle of ketchup.

Geraldine shrieked and ran behind me. It was one of the oddest things I'd ever seen.

"What's going on?" I asked.

Ava cocked her head to the side. "You're her best friend, Bex. Surely you know about her stupid ketchup phobia."

I looked back at Geraldine as she crouched lower behind me. "You're afraid of ketchup?"

"Yes," she whispered.

"Geraldine, why are you afraid of ketchup?" I asked.

"I just am. It's all thick and red like blood. It creeps me out."

The girl proceeded to chase Geraldine with the bottle of ketchup. Geraldine ran around the room screaming and everyone burst into giggles. A silver bowl with some kind of beige-colored batter sat on another counter. Geraldine grabbed it.

"I got batter and I'm not afraid to use it. This will never come out of that beautiful dress," Geraldine warned.

The girl paused. "You wouldn't."

Geraldine didn't look like she was joking to me. "Take one more step and I will."

The girl took another step and Geraldine fulfilled her promise. She grabbed a spoon from the counter and slung a giant glob of batter on the girl's dress.

"You idiot!" the girl screamed. The other girls screeched like they'd just seen a giant hairy tarantula.

Geraldine looked at everyone else. "You all think this is funny? You can get some too." She ran around the room flinging batter at the girls as they scurried away from her, shrieking. I crouched underneath a counter, hoping not to get hit.

"Girls, what is going on in here?" That was Carol's voice. The room fell silent. I came out from under the counter. Batter was everywhere. I was happy to see some dripping from Ava's hair, but Carol was livid, so I hid my smile. "You girls have totally wrecked this kitchen. I can't believe this. I have Silver Roses in here all the time helping out and I've never had a problem. Now the lunches aren't made and we have a mess to clean up. Thanks a lot!"

"It was all her fault," Summer said, pointing at Geraldine, who was still foolishly holding the bowl of batter.

Carol sighed and shook her head. "That was batter for a birthday cake for one of the children." My heart sank like a stone. We had totally messed up, or they had. I hadn't done anything wrong, but the whole thing had started with Geraldine trying to stick up for me. "I'll have to call Mrs. Armstrong and tell her how you all have represented this organization and that you won't be welcomed back."

"Please don't do that," Summer whined.

"I don't have a choice. Get this kitchen cleaned up," Carol said before storming out. I couldn't blame her. She had every right to be furious.

"Thanks a lot, you freak!" Ava yelled at Geraldine. "Now we're all probably going to get kicked out of the program."

"Do you see now why everyone hates you?" Summer asked.

They weren't exactly innocent in all this. They shouldn't have been chasing her with ketchup, but Geraldine shouldn't have thrown the batter all over the kitchen.

Hannah pulled off her gloves and hairnet. "I'm not spending my Saturday cleaning up the mess you made. Clean it up yourself," she told Geraldine.

The other girls followed suit and headed out of the kitchen. Amber looked at me. "Come on, Bex. I told you this girl was bad news."

I took my hairnet and gloves off also. The little Bex on my right shoulder was telling me to stay and help Geraldine clean up. The little Bex on my left shoulder told me to follow Amber. She was my chance to actually have a normal friend in the Silver Roses and this was mostly Geraldine's fault anyway.

Geraldine grabbed a dishcloth from the sink as I followed Amber out the door. I knew I would hate myself for the rest of the day.

Aunt Jeanie pulled into the parking lot and I slid onto the front seat.

"I heard there was a food fight. What did you do?" Boy, did word travel fast.

"I didn't do anything." I guess I couldn't really blame her for assuming, because disasters were usually my fault, but this one time it actually wasn't me.

Aunt Jeanie looked relieved. "Are you sure?"

"Yes, Aunt Jeanie." But I wasn't sure. I hadn't done anything wrong as far as messing up the kitchen, but my conscience was definitely bothering me about something else.

8

Giving Back—Take Two

—feeling smart ☺

<u>Junior Silver Rose Candidate Response Journal Page 13</u>
What quote or poem inspires you and why?
I refuse to join any club that would have me as a
member.—Groucho Marx
—Self-explanatory

Aunt Jeanie thought she would thoroughly destroy my
weekend by making me babysit the Brat Squad Sunday
afternoon while she dragged Uncle Bob furniture shopping.
My community service project had to be completed within
a week and I needed to come up with something else to do.

The second my aunt and uncle walked out the door, Reagan and Francois began sliding down the stairs on a boogie-board while Priscilla and Penelope argued over who had ripped a unicorn poster. I needed to find something for these kids to do and I had a great idea. I needed to perform a service for the community and I had four little monsters who needed to be occupied.

"Hey, guys, let's play a game," I yelled up the stairs.

Francois froze where he stood, holding the boogie board. "What kind of game?"

"We're going to see who can win the best citizen contest." I paused to wait for their reactions. I'd learned that you could get them to do anything by turning it into a contest.

"If I don't win, it will be a calamity," Ray announced. *Calamity* was Ray's word of the week at school, which meant we had to hear it at least one hundred times a day.

"How do you win?" Penelope asked.

"Follow me," I told the kids as I led them to the kitchen. I found a pen and sheet of paper in a drawer and made a list of several senior citizens in our neighborhood. Helping the elderly was always smiled upon. "I'm going to give you a job to do for someone. You're going to go to their house and do it and have them sign this piece of paper. The

66

person who does the best job will get an awesome surprise."

"What's the surprise?" Penelope asked suspiciously.

"It's a surprise," I answered because I had no idea what I would give them.

"Penelope and Priscilla, you're going to take the Washingtons' dogs, Fifi, Bebe, and GiGi, for a nice long walk. Francois, you can water the Thompsons' plants. Ray, you will help Mrs. Avery do whatever she needs done around the house."

I needed them out of the house for an hour so I could have sixty minutes of peace. I didn't think that was too much to ask out of my weekend.

"Okay, but I don't do windows," Ray said.

After listening to the four of them arguing about who was going to win the contest as they walked down the walkway, I poured myself a glass of lemonade and sat on the swinging bench on the front porch listening to music through my headphones. Soon, I drifted off to sleep.

My friends and I were whitewater rafting down the Amazon River when someone interrupted my dream.

"Excuse me," said a deep voice.

I opened my eyes to see a police officer standing over me. "Huh?" I closed my eyes and opened them again. Was I still dreaming?

"Do you know this child?" the officer asked.

I sat up to see Ray and Mrs. Avery standing behind him. "Yeah, she's my little sister. What's wrong?"

"She came into my house while I was napping upstairs—just walked right in. I heard a noise downstairs so I called the police," Mrs. Avery explained.

I looked at my little sister. "Ray, you know you're supposed to knock before going into someone's house."

"Well, the door was open," Ray whined. "You should lock your doors, Mrs. Avery. Anybody can just walk right in."

Before Mrs. Avery could respond, Mr. Washington came barreling down the walk with Priscilla and Penelope on his heels. A lump formed in my throat when I noticed the three pink leashes in his hand with no dogs attached.

He looked at the policeman. "I'm glad you're here, Officer. These little hooligans took my dogs for a walk and then let them get away. I want them arrested for animal endangerment."

The officer put his hands on his hips. "Sir, I can't arrest them for losing your dogs."

"It was all Penelope's fault," Priscilla said. "She wanted to take their leashes off and make the dogs have a race but they kept running and running and they never came back."

Penelope looked at Mr. Washington. "I told them to stop at the stop sign. You really should train your dogs to listen."

Mr. Washington turned bright red, but not as red as Mrs. Thompson when she stepped onto the porch dragging Francois by his sleeve. "He flooded my living room!"

"Francois, you didn't," I moaned.

Francois shrugged. "I was just trying to help. I watered the outside plants, and then I wanted to water the inside plants too, so I could win the contest."

"What contest?" the officer asked.

"Bex said we were having a helping contest so we were trying to do nice things for people," Ray answered.

The officer shook his head. "I'm going to need the number of a responsible adult."

"Mommy's here!" Francois yelled.

"Oh no," Ray said. "This is going to be a calamity!" She was right about that.

Our disgruntled neighbors continued to complain to the police officer and the Brat Squad argued with each other about who should win the contest. I slipped inside the house before Aunt Jeanie could make it to the porch. Upstairs I made one final entry in my journal because I knew I was about to die. I had written two paragraphs when the bedroom door swung open.

"What on earth were you thinking?" Aunt Jeanie demanded. "We're gone for a little over an hour and we come home to a police car in our driveway?"

I sat up on the bed. "I'm sorry—"

"And what was this contest about?"

"I was just teaching the kids how to give back to the community," I told her.

"Really? Or were you trying to get them to do your community service project?"

"Aunt Jeanie! I'm insulted by that accusation!"

She raised her one eyebrow at me. "You will never babysit again."

That was supposed to be a punishment?

"Aww, Aunt Jeanie, give me one more chance," I pretend-begged.

"Absolutely not!"

She slammed the door and I breathed a sigh of relief. Trust me. I won't lose any sleep over not being able to babysit the Brat Squad.

Bex: 2　　　　　　**Aunt Jeanie: 3**

9

Eating With Sharks

—feeling overwhelmed ☹

Junior Silver Rose Candidate Response Journal Page 16

Why is it important to demonstrate proper etiquette when dining?

Because Aunt Jeanie gives me dirty looks if I don't.

One of our classes took place at a restaurant. Mrs. Armstrong had reserved a room just for us. We sat at a long table covered with a white tablecloth set with lots of plates and silverware. Aunt Jeanie had made me take an etiquette class before, but I didn't remember too much of what I had learned. I just knew it seemed like a lot of work and rules just to eat. Eating should be fun, not a chore.

I sat between Geraldine and Amber. First Mrs. Armstrong went over all the plates and utensils on the table. She told us what they were called and what they were used for. Most of the girls seemed bored; they already knew this stuff. I tried to remember as much as possible so I didn't make a fool out of myself. Geraldine, on the other hand, was balancing her silverware on the bottom of an upside-down teacup.

Mrs. Armstrong cleared her throat and glared at Geraldine who quickly put everything back the way it was supposed to be.

We placed our napkins in our laps. I didn't stuff my napkin in my collar. I remembered that my glass was the one on my right. I sipped my soup instead of slurping it.

Mrs. Armstrong walked around making notes on her clipboard. I cut my salad once before picking it up with my spoon. I learned it was rude to cut more than once before taking a bite.

Mrs. Armstrong bent over me. "The sharp part of your knife should not be pointing outward, dear. That's aggressive."

I sighed and turned the pointy part inward. It seemed like no matter how much I learned there was something else I didn't know.

When Amber asked for the salt, I handed her the salt and the pepper together. I buttered my bread one bite at a time. I hoped Mrs. Armstrong was taking note of this.

I discovered that Geraldine was an awfully slow eater. One of the rules of etiquette was to eat at the same pace as everyone else so that you would be ready for the next course. I watched her as she cut her peas in half. I had never seen anyone do that before.

I leaned over to her. "Geraldine, you might want to eat a little faster."

"I can't. My digestive system is very sensitive. It can only handle a little bit of food at a time."

As I predicted, everyone finished her meal except for Geraldine.

"Hurry up so we can have dessert, idiot," Summer whispered from across the table.

I wished Mrs. Armstrong had heard that, but of course she hadn't.

"Oh, relax. I'm almost done," Geraldine said too loudly. But she wasn't almost done. Her plate was still full.

The girls stared at Geraldine impatiently, but she didn't care. Finally she pushed her plate away from her, which was not proper etiquette. "Okay, I'm done!"

"Shhh," hissed Mrs. Armstrong. "You don't have to be so loud."

Our dinner plates were cleared and we were served dessert, cheesecake with strawberries. I was enjoying a nice conversation with Amber when Geraldine shrieked.

I looked over to see a syrup-covered strawberry sitting on her lap. "Who did that?" she demanded, hopping up from the table.

I looked around the table. Mrs. Armstrong had left the room. The other girls went back to eating, but I noticed a few of them smirking.

"Geraldine, just forget it. Sit down," I said gently.

"I won't! I'm afraid of strawberries and they might flick another one at me."

"What? Are you afraid of all red foods?" Amber asked.

"Red foods that look like blood," Geraldine answered.

Summer flicked another strawberry at her. Geraldine screamed and ran around the table. Mrs. Armstrong came back in to see what the commotion was. "Geraldine Ulysses! What is your problem?"

"They're assaulting me with strawberries," she answered.

"Mrs. Armstrong, what is she talking about?" Summer asked innocently.

Mrs. Armstrong took a deep breath. "I have no idea what she's talking about. Sit down, Geraldine."

If there was ever a time for her to get over her red-food phobia it was that moment. She looked like a crazy person.

Geraldine shook her head and stomped her foot like a child. "I'm calling my mother to come and get me. I refuse to be victimized."

She left the room, I guess to call her mother, and everyone at the table started talking about her, which I knew wasn't good etiquette.

"See what I told you?" Amber said. "Disaster. That girl messes up everything we do."

I hated to agree with Amber on that point, but I had to. Geraldine was a liability and I needed to lose her ASAP.

10

Fake Friends

—feeling annoyed ☹

<u>Junior Silver Rose Candidate Response Journal Page 18</u>
If you could embark on any business venture, what
would it be?

I would open a sports center where girls could go and play
any kind of sports they wanted. There'd be a football field,
basketball court, baseball diamond, soccer field, swimming
pool, golf court, tennis court, and track. No boys would be
allowed! I like boys and everything, but I feel if they were
around, girls would be more focused on trying to impress
them instead of playing sports.

There would also be a bakery attached to the sports center that made every kind of cupcake known to man— but their specialty would be red velvet cupcakes with cream cheese frosting.

I was actually looking forward to Tuesday's Silver Rose meeting because it was about women in business. I'd much rather learn about being an independent woman earning her own money than talking about eye shadow. I wanted to be like Aunt Alice. She made her own living and didn't answer to anyone.

I wasn't looking forward to seeing Geraldine. I had felt guilty about ditching her all weekend and I didn't know how she would react to seeing me.

Five minutes before class started and Geraldine wasn't there. She had arrived super early for all the previous classes so I figured maybe she wasn't coming. Maybe she'd quit the group. I would have. I was having a nice conversation with Amber about a new movie that was coming out when Geraldine walked in wearing a camouflage vest and carrying a hot pink gift bag.

The girls stopped talking and watched Geraldine. The silence turned to murmuring and giggles. I thought maybe

Geraldine had brought Mrs. Armstrong a present to apologize for her behavior at the soup kitchen. But no. It wasn't for Mrs. Armstrong at all. Geraldine marched over and held the gift bag out to me. Amber disappeared from my side.

Reluctantly I took the bag from Geraldine. "Uh, what's this for?"

"You're my best friend and I wanted to do something nice for you," Geraldine answered.

"Oh. Thanks," I said, putting the bag underneath my seat.

"Bex, open it," Ava called from across the room. Have I mentioned how much I can't stand this girl?

"Yeah, open it, Bex," Geraldine insisted.

All eyes were on me. Even Mrs. Armstrong, who had just taken the podium, looked on expectantly.

I had a sick feeling that whatever I pulled from the bag was going to be weird and embarrassing. I reached in and pulled out a humongous vest with a soccer ball print. Yep, weird and embarrassing. I should be a psychic.

Laughter filled the room. I felt like I was in a room of hyenas. Geraldine grinned from ear to ear. "Like it, Bex?"

"It's so . . . different. I can honestly say I've never had a vest covered with soccer balls."

"Yay," Geraldine said, squeezing my arm. "Wear it to the next meeting. We can be vest twins."

More laughter from the hyenas.

Mrs. Armstrong banged her gavel on the podium. "Ladies, let's come to order."

We all took our seats. Of course, Geraldine sat right next to me.

"Before we get started with today's class, something needs to be addressed. I got a very disheartening phone call this weekend from Carol at the soup kitchen. She told me about the fiasco that occurred and that our Silver Roses wouldn't be welcomed back. It took a great deal of talking, but I got her to give us another chance. I shouldn't have to remind you that you are representing us everywhere you go and we will not tolerate this kind of nonsense. The culprit will have twenty-five points deducted from her final score."

Everyone stared at Geraldine, who was still smiling from ear to ear. Didn't she realize Mrs. Armstrong was talking about her? Twenty-five was a lot of points; Geraldine would probably never recover from that.

"But," Mrs. Armstrong continued, "Carol also told me that Geraldine was the only one who stayed to clean up the mess, so I am giving her an additional ten points and deducting ten from the rest of you who were present. Bad form, ladies."

The girls shot Geraldine dirty looks.

"But she made the mess to begin with!" Summer complained.

"So what?" asked Mrs. Armstrong. "You were there for the purposes of serving those women and children. Leaving the way you did hurt no one but them. It doesn't matter who caused the mess, you should have stayed and helped clean for their sake. That doesn't say very much for your character."

She had a good point. I didn't even mind that I was getting ten points deducted. Leaving the kitchen a mess, even if I hadn't caused it, was selfish.

"Ms. Ulysses, even though you caused the mess, I commend you for spending the rest of the afternoon there fixing your mistake," Mrs. Armstrong said.

I patted Geraldine on the shoulder. I figured a girl like her didn't get many compliments.

No one argued any further, but I knew Geraldine would pay for the point deductions later.

The business seminar was interesting but it was hard to concentrate with Geraldine constantly whispering in my ear. I did perk back up when Mrs. Armstrong mentioned something about an overnight retreat. I was all for slumber parties, but with people I liked, not these awful girls. Maybe I could fake a stomachache or something to get out of it.

The following school day the inevitable happened. All of a sudden, Ava G. and Kristen were all buddy-buddy. I mean they walked through the hallways with their arms looped together as if they'd been best friends their whole lives. They ate lunch together. They laughed and joked with each other all throughout PE.

"It's nice to see that you and Ava are friends now, but I have to say I'm a little surprised," I told Kristen when I ran into her in the restroom.

"I'm not friends with that jerk. I hate her just as much as you do, probably more," Kristen said smirking.

"That's not what it looks like to me."

Kristen checked her eyebrows in the mirror. "Trust me, Bex. Keep your friends close and your enemies closer. I'm just pretending to be her friend and when she lets her guard down—wham!" Kristen pounded her fist into her hand.

"What does *wham* mean?" I asked.

"What do you think? I'm gonna kick her butt. Nobody in this school will respect her after that."

Kristen zipped her purse and put it on her shoulder. "And don't you dare tell anyone I told you this."

I sighed as she left the bathroom. I'd seen a few fights since I'd been at Lincoln Middle. Kids got excited about them, but not me. As much as I couldn't stand Ava, I didn't think I really wanted to see her get beaten up.

11

Sleepover Frenemies

—feeling traumatized ☹

<u>Junior Silver Rose Candidate Response Journal Page 21</u>
The Silver Rose Foundation is an institution of sisterhood. Discuss how you have connected with fellow pledges.

They don't like me and the feeling is mutual.

Apparently it was some sort of great privilege to hold the annual Junior Silver Rose Retreat at your house. Mrs. Groves had been granted the honors this year, so because the universe hates me I would have to spend the night with Ava G.

When Mrs. Armstrong said we were going on a retreat, I was thinking more along the lines of camping or doing something outdoors. I should have known these girls would never do something like that.

Friday night I lay on the bed doubled over, clutching my stomach.

"Ray," I said in the weakest voice I could manage, "please go tell Aunt Jeanie that I'm dying. Hurry, I don't have much time left."

Ray ran from the room. "Aunt Jeanie, Bex is dying!" she yelled down the hallway.

Aunt Jeanie took an awful long time to come, considering I was on my deathbed. She stood over me and raised one eyebrow. "What is it, Bex?"

"My stomach and my head and my throat—they all hurt," I answered.

"Right. Are you sure you aren't just doing this to get out of the retreat?" Aunt Jeanie asked suspiciously.

"No. I've been looking forward to this all week."

Aunt Jeanie folded her arms across her chest. "Fine. I'll make your Nana's special home remedy and then we'll take you to the emergency room."

"The emergency room?"

"Yes," Aunt Jeanie answered. "If you're dying I think that qualifies as an emergency. Now I just need to run to the grocery store to pick up some cod liver oil, beets, bean sprouts, soy sauce, and liverwurst for the home remedy."

Okay. She wasn't buying my story.

Bex: 2   **Aunt Jeanie: 4**

I jumped up from the bed. "It's a miracle! The pain just went away."

"That's what I thought," Aunt Jeanie said. "Let's go."

Aunt Jeanie felt the need to lecture me the entire way to the Groves' house. She was acting as if I had never been out of the house before. "Bex, please, none of your shenanigans and hijinks."

Hijinks? What were hijinks?

"Bex, are you listening to me?"

"Yes, Aunt Jeanie." But I wasn't. I was too busy thinking about how horrible this night was going to be.

"Bex, this is a big night and a good time for you to network and bond with the other girls. Please just be nice and act . . . normal," Aunt Jeanie said, as we pulled into the driveway.

"What does that mean? I always act normal."

"It means no telling any of your horrible scary stories. Do not start a food fight and do not get any of your bright ideas. Got it?"

"Sure, Aunt Jeanie," I sighed. I figured if I sat in a corner and kept to myself I couldn't do anything wrong.

Twenty girls swarmed into Ava's enormous living room with their sleeping bags. Everyone was there except for Geraldine. We had pizza and fudge sundaes and then we were to spend the rest of the night bonding with our "sisters."

"If you girls need anything," Mrs. Groves said as she headed up the stairs, "tell Mildred. Good night."

Mildred, the housekeeper, was busy cleaning up the kitchen. We were left on our own.

The doorbell rang and Ava ran to answer it. "Look who's here," she said as she reentered the living room. Surprisingly she seemed happy to see Geraldine.

Geraldine wore pajamas with carrots on them that also looked homemade. "Sorry I'm late. I was at my Alien Invasion Preparedness meeting. Tonight we were discussing how to build a shelter if the aliens decide to take over."

Silence.

"Wow," Ava said. "That's so interesting. You have to tell us all about it, but later. Come on."

Why was Ava being so nice to her?

Summer moved over on her sleeping bag. "Geraldine, come sit next to me."

Geraldine beamed, laid down her duffle bag, and sat beside her. Something weird was going on.

"Geraldine," Summer said, "you got us all in a lot of trouble the other day and I think it's only fair that you make it up to us."

"How can I do that?" Geraldine asked.

Summer continued. "My older sister was a Junior Silver Rose. She told me that it's tradition that the pledges pull a prank on Mrs. Armstrong the night of the retreat. She only lives two blocks from here. We think you should do it. It will help restore your standing with us."

Geraldine frowned. "I don't know. That sounds really risky."

Hannah sat on the other side of Geraldine. "You will go down in Silver Rose history as a legend. The girl who pulls the prank always turns out to be the most popular."

"What if I get caught?" Geraldine asked.

"*Don't* get caught," Ava replied.

Geraldine sighed, taking it all in.

"Are you going to do it or not?" Summer asked impatiently. "Because if you're not, any other girl in this room would love to take your place." Summer looked around the room. "Who'd like to do it instead?"

Everyone's hands shot up except for mine and Amber's.

"No, I'll do it," Geraldine said confidently. "What's the prank?" That might have been a good question to ask before committing to it.

Summer hugged her knees to her chest. "Every year they pull the same pranks, they either egg or t.p. Armstrong's house. She's expecting it. This year we need to do something special, something that's going to make history."

"W-what's that?" Geraldine stammered.

Hannah pulled a heavy plastic bag from her duffle. "You're going to spray paint her lawn silver."

"That's going to make her really mad and she already doesn't like me," Geraldine said.

"No, it's not," Ava said. "Trust us. Mrs. Armstrong is a good sport."

"Geraldine, don't do it," I said.

Summer looked at me sharply. "Shut up, Bex."

"I'll do it if she doesn't want to," said a girl named Carly.

"No, no. I'll do it. I'll do it," Geraldine relented. "But I don't want to be out there by myself."

"Don't worry," Ava said. "Some of us will go with you."

Geraldine looked at me. "Bex, will you come?"

Aunt Jeanie's warning echoed in my mind. *Just be normal. Don't do anything stupid.* "Geraldine, I don't really want to—"

"Please," she pleaded.

"All right, all right." I guessed it would be a good idea for me to go and make sure things didn't get out of control.

Ava, Summer, Hannah, Geraldine, and I put our sneakers on.

"What do we tell your mom if she comes down and wants to know where you guys are?" Carly asked Ava.

"Mom is off duty," Ava answered. "She won't come down unless there's a fire or something and Mildred doesn't care what we do as long as we're quiet. Come on."

She handed the bag of spray paint to Geraldine and we were off.

The streets were quiet as we walked to the Armstrong's house, almost too quiet, like something bad was about to happen. Even with the glow of the streetlights, it was still too dark for me. Scenes from scary movies played in my mind. I shivered.

Geraldine and I lagged behind the other girls.

"Geraldine, you don't have to do this," I whispered to her as we crossed the street.

"I have to," Geraldine answered. "Maybe then the girls will accept me."

"No, Geraldine. They won't. No matter what you do they'll never be nice to you. They're using you."

"Don't worry, Bex. No matter what happens, you'll still be my best friend. You don't have to be afraid of me making new ones."

This girl was seriously clueless. "No, Geraldine, I . . ."

"There's her house," Summer announced. "Don't worry; we'll be hiding behind the shrubs over there." Summer pointed to a row of tall shrubs that lined the edge of the yard.

Geraldine nodded and headed for Mrs. Armstrong's lawn. I felt sorry for her in her carrot pajamas, having no idea what was really going on.

I followed the other girls and stood behind the shrubs. Mrs. Armstrong's house was ginormous. Her house was even bigger than Aunt Jeanie's. There was one light on upstairs. I figured that was the bedroom. The rest of the house was dark.

Geraldine went to the far end of the yard and removed a can of spray paint from the bag. She shook it and began to spray.

"She's such an idiot," Ava said, taking out her phone to record Geraldine's act of vandalism.

"You guys are going to get her into so much trouble," I said.

"So what?" Hannah replied. "She got us in trouble at the soup kitchen, it's not like she's ever going to become a Silver Rose anyway. She's totally wasting her time."

Geraldine slowly made her way up and down the huge yard carefully spraying the grass. It would take her forever to complete it and there wasn't nearly enough spray paint.

"Hey, guys!" Geraldine yelled from across the lawn. "How about I spray a rose in the grass? That would be cool, right?"

I cringed. The light on upstairs meant the Armstrongs were still awake. Geraldine was about to get us all caught.

"O-M-G," Hannah moaned.

"Shhhh," Summer hissed, but Geraldine kept screaming at the top of her lungs.

"Well, what do you guys think?"

My heart dropped into my stomach as a light from downstairs clicked on. We ducked behind the hedges and froze.

"Who's out there?" called a man's voice.

I couldn't see him and I couldn't see Geraldine. I heard the door close and I peeked over the hedges. "He went back inside," I whispered, ducking back down.

At that moment something went shk-shk-shk and Geraldine screamed. We all stood to see what was happening. Someone had turned the sprinklers on and Geraldine was getting soaked.

The door flew open and I heard Mrs. Armstrong's voice followed by a dog's vicious barking. "Get 'em, Killer!"

"Killer!" Ava screamed and we all took off running down the street with a soggy Geraldine trailing behind us.

I was faster than all the other girls. I had no intentions of being gobbled up by a dog named Killer. We stopped running when we got to Ava's street and Killer was nowhere in sight. We walked back to the house at a normal pace.

"So, did I prove myself to the sisterhood?" Geraldine asked.

Hannah turned to her. "Are you kidding me? Your yelling woke them up, you moron. We got chased down the street by a dog because of you."

Geraldine frowned and looked down at the ground. Hopefully what I had told her before about the girls not being her friends was starting to settle in.

Inside all the other girls wanted to know what had happened. Ava was giving them the gory details when a knock on the door interrupted her. It was Mrs. Armstrong. She had on a black bathrobe and her hair was in curlers. I chuckled to myself because I was used to seeing her look absolutely perfect.

We all sat on our sleeping bags looking as innocent as possible except for Geraldine who still stood awkwardly by the door, dripping wet.

Mrs. Armstrong cleared her throat. "Someone has just vandalized my lawn with spray paint. Silver spray paint. Since I know it's a tradition for the Silver Roses to pull a prank on me on the night of the retreat, I'm going to assume it was one of you. More specifically, the one who's soaking wet right now." All eyes went to Geraldine. She looked at the ground and said nothing. What could she possibly say to defend herself? She even had silver spray paint on her fingers.

Mrs. Armstrong looked her up and down. "Young lady, this is your second strike and that's two strikes too many. Your bid to become a Junior Silver Rose is for the *second* time hereby revoked."

Geraldine's shoulders drooped, but most of the girls were smirking. This had been their plan all along and they had accomplished it.

"I will let your mother know in the morning," Mrs. Armstrong said. "I'm sure she will be very embarrassed and disappointed."

Mrs. Armstrong turned to leave, but I had a very important question. "Wait, Mrs. Armstrong. If you knew it was one of us pulling a prank, why did you sic your dog on us? We could have gotten killed."

She dug in her pocket and pulled out something that looked like a silver remote control. She pressed a button and the sound of a dog barking filled the room. "We don't have a dog," she answered. "But I'm curious, Rebecca. You asked, 'Why did you sic your dog on *us*?' Who is the 'us' you are referring too?"

A lump rose in my throat. *Nice going, Bex.*

"Um, um, um," I stammered. I was totally not a good liar.

Mrs. Armstrong glared at me. "Were you there with Geraldine, Rebecca?"

"Yes, but I didn't spray paint anything and I told her not to do it," I answered honestly.

Mrs. Armstrong folded her arms across her chest. "Who else was there, Rebecca?"

I weighed my options. I glanced at Ava and she gave me the look of death. Geraldine and I were already in trouble regardless. There really wasn't any need to drag anyone else into it. On the other hand, the people who were really at fault would be getting away with murder. Why should I protect them?

So, I sang like a canary. "Ava, Summer, and Hannah. They were there too. The whole thing was actually their idea."

The other girls gasped, probably thinking I was the stupidest person in the world.

"Oh, really," Mrs. Armstrong said looking at the other girls. I secretly hoped she would kick us all out of the group. She would be doing me a favor; however, I wouldn't get my new bedroom. "Each of you will be getting ten points deducted and I will be speaking to your mothers in the morning."

I thought she had let them off way too easily, but she

was friends with their moms. I was sure that had something to do with it.

Mrs. Armstrong left and the room buzzed with conversation.

"Bex Carter, you've done it now," Ava said. "I didn't think it was possible to hate you any more than I already did, but I do. *I hate you, I hate you, I hate you!*"

"How could you snitch on your sisters like that?" Hannah asked.

I narrowed my eyes at Hannah to show I wasn't afraid of them. "Are you guys kidding me? You're not my sisters. You're not even nice to me."

Geraldine went into the bathroom to change into some dry clothes and more girls yelled at me for being a snitch and a traitor. I rolled over in my sleeping bag and tried to block them out. "You'd better sleep with one eye open," was the last thing I heard.

Despite the horrible night that had transpired, I slept peacefully. At some point during the night Geraldine had shaken me awake, but I shooed her away. When I opened my eyes the next morning it took me a few seconds to remember that I was at Ava's house and not in my bed at Aunt Jeanie's. Something hanging from the staircase banister caught my eye. Underwear. Black underwear with white polka dots from a fancy boutique. *My* underwear.

Slowly I sat up in my sleeping bag. Several other girls were already sitting up talking. Some of them giggled when they saw that I was awake.

"She's up," someone whispered.

Ava came down the stairs fully dressed. "Oh, Bex, you're up. We did a little decorating while you were sleeping. She reached the bottom of the stairs and stood under my underwear. "I heard your aunt telling my mother how awful it was to shop for you because you're humongous." She pointed to the hanging undergarments. "I mean look at the size of those things. Where do you even find underwear that big? I could use them as a parachute." She was totally exaggerating. Yes, I was tall and big-boned, but I was nowhere near the gigantic monster she was making me out to be.

The room erupted in laughter. I ran up the stairs and began to untie my things from the banister.

"The best part is that I took pictures," Ava said waving her pink phone back and forth. "I've sent them to everyone at school."

My face felt warm; I knew it was beet red. I wanted to cry, but I wouldn't. Not in front of these girls.

I didn't speak to anyone as we ate French toast for breakfast and then changed into our clothes. There were eight bathrooms in the Groves' house, but with twenty-one girls, it still wasn't enough. In one of the upstairs bathrooms, someone was in the shower and Amber stood in front of the mirror brushing her hair. I stood beside her to tackle my own.

"Sorry about that underwear thing," Amber said. "That was harsh, but I told you to stay away from Geraldine. She's a disaster. If you want to be a Junior Silver Rose, you cannot be friends with her."

The shower cut off.

"I'm not friends with her. She just latched on to me and I can't get rid of her. I only went with her last night because I felt sorry for her."

The shower curtain flew open and Geraldine stepped out wrapped in a towel. "That's good to know, Bex. Thanks for pretending to be my friend. I really thought there was something different about you, but it's good to know you're a mean girl just like the rest of them."

No, I wasn't a mean girl. "Geraldine, I—"

"Save it. I got kicked out, remember? By the way, I tried to warn you last night about the underwear, but you wouldn't listen to me. Don't worry. You don't have to deal

with me *latching* onto you anymore. Have a nice life."
Geraldine brushed past me as she left the bathroom. I had
to be the most horrible person in the world.

Amber put her hand on my shoulder. "Forget about that,
Bex. It's easier this way. She needed to know the truth."

But Amber was wrong. I had been honest, but
something I had done was wrong, because I hurt a girl who
only wanted to be my friend.

I slammed the door after I got into Aunt Jeanie's
Mercedes.

"What's with you?" she asked. "I mean besides losing
ten points. Mrs. Armstrong called me this morning. Bex, I
told you—"

"You know, Aunt Jeanie, I really don't care about that
right now. Did you or did you not have a discussion with
Mrs. Groves about bra shopping for me?"

Aunt Jeanie frowned. "What? Bex, what does that have
to do with anything?"

Aunt Jeanie had hurt me a lot, but how was I supposed
to trust her if she was going to go around town telling
everyone my business? I already had it bad enough with
Ava. I didn't need Aunt Jeanie giving her any more
ammunition.

"I don't know what you're talking about."

I wasn't about to let her play stupid with me. "Ava, the one you think is so sweet and charming, the one you want me to be like. Do you know what she did? While I was sleeping, she hung my underwear from the banister. Everybody laughed at how big they were and Ava said she overheard you talking to Mrs. Groves about underwear shopping for me. Aunt Jeanie, how could you do that?"

She sighed. "Bex, it's not like that, okay. This teenager thing is new to me and sometimes Mrs. Groves and I compare notes, that's all. We ask each other for advice. It's not like I'm gossiping about you. And what Ava did, I'm sure was just a harmless slumber party prank. Don't take it so seriously."

But that prank wasn't fun or lighthearted at all. It was meant to be cruel. Aunt Jeanie hadn't heard how those girls laughed at me.

"I heard about Geraldine having her application for membership revoked. I told you to stay away from that girl. She's bad news."

I sat back in my seat and stared out the window. "Don't worry about it. I'm pretty sure she'll never speak to me again."

"By the way, next week you all start ballroom dancing

lessons. You need to choose a partner. Uncle Bob is not much of a dancer, but I'm sure he'll be willing to do it if we ask."

Of course . . . because this day wasn't bad enough already. I had been dreading this part of the program. Most of the girls were having their fathers as their escorts, but my dad was in prison. I tried really hard not to get angry with my parents for not being around, but times like this made it hard.

12

Dancing With Wolves

—feeling hopeless ☹

Junior Silver Rose Candidate Response Journal Page 23
Who have you chosen to be your escort at the
Coronation ceremony and why?

I have chosen Austin Jeffrey. Austin is my friend who is a boy. He is NOT my boyfriend because if I had a boyfriend Aunt Jeanie would ship me off to a boarding school. I chose Austin because he's really nice and Chirpy says he's good arm candy.

I had been dreading going to school Monday considering Ava had texted a picture of my underwear to everyone, but surprisingly no one said anything about it. For some reason Ava must not have sent the picture like she'd said and I wasn't going to be dumb enough to ask her about it.

Tuesday was our first class minus Geraldine. I had thought about her all weekend. Part of me wanted to call her, but then I figured it was best to leave things the way they were.

None of the girls were talking to me except for Amber because I was a snitch. I had warned Austin that we would be walking into a snake pit, but he didn't care. He said he just wanted to be there for me.

Imagine everyone's surprise when I walked in with such a cutie on my arm. I thought Austin was adorable. He has shaggy brown hair, big brown eyes, and dimples. The only thing is that he is shorter than me, but that really isn't his fault. I'm just way tall. I hoped he would hit a growth spurt soon and then everything would even out.

I held my head up high as Austin led me to an empty seat. The room had been cleared to accommodate a dance floor. The chairs formed a U shape around the room. We received lots of stares and whispers. Everyone was probably jealous. Yes, they had their fathers with them, but I had the cutest guy in the room.

A man named Mr. Steve was our dance instructor. He showed us how to do a simple waltz and a few other ballroom dances. Dancing was definitely not a talent of mine, but it was hard to be bad at it with Austin leading me.

This wasn't the first time I'd danced with Austin. He had accompanied me to my Valentine's Dance last year. That was how we met. His mother was a friend of Aunt Jeanie's, so I guess I owed meeting Austin to my aunt.

At first my cheeks felt warm as Austin placed his hand on my back, but I got used to it. I have to admit we were pretty good, but we probably still needed a lot of practice (wink, wink).

The best part of the class happened when class was actually over.

"How much did Bex have to pay you to be her partner?" Summer asked Austin.

"It's the other way around. I'm actually paying her to *let* me be her partner. A million bucks a day and I think I'm getting a pretty good deal." See why I liked him so much, I mean a little bit?

That shut Summer up. She huffed away and left us alone.

Austin took my hand. "I'm glad you're not like them. I can't stand girls like that. That's the thing I like most about you, Bex, your heart."

I blushed, but I wondered if he would still feel that way if he knew about the way I had treated Geraldine.

The next day I sat in the living room trying to do math homework I didn't understand. I was good with math as long as it dealt with numbers, but once you threw letters in the mix, it became foreign to me.

Aunt Jeanie, Mrs. Groves, and Mrs. Campbell who lived down the street were having tea at the dining room table. The three of them had just come from playing tennis. They discussed everyone they had seen at the country club that day, including what they had done and said. All three of them had too much time on their hands.

Finally Mrs. Campbell announced she had to leave because she and her husband were going to a dinner party that night and she needed to get ready.

Mrs. Groves took another sip of her tea. "How long is she going to carry that bag? It's three seasons old already."

"I think Kevin tightened the purse strings," Aunt Jeanie replied. "Her real problem is the weight she's gaining. She seems bigger every time I see her."

105

"She's definitely letting herself go," Mrs. Groves agreed. "And if she tells us one more time about her trip to Saint-Tropez . . ."

The two of them cackled like witches. I imagined they had been the mean girls when they were in middle school.

"You shouldn't do that," I blurted out.

"Excuse me?" Mrs. Groves asked.

"You shouldn't be nice to someone to her face and then say mean things about her behind her back. Mrs. Campbell thinks you're her friends," I said.

Aunt Jeanie gave Mrs. Groves a look, then she turned to me. "Bex, this is an adult conversation."

"Yeah? I couldn't tell," I replied.

Mrs. Groves gasped and Aunt Jeanie shot up from the table. "Go to your room right now!" she said in her scary whisper.

I stomped up the stairs. I hadn't meant to be rude, but I knew I was right this time. I also knew that I needed to take my own advice. I'd accused Ava, Kristen, Aunt Jeanie, and Mrs. Groves of being fake friends when I was guilty of the same thing. I stopped at the phone in the hallway and dialed Geraldine's number. The phone rang a long time before going to voicemail. "Listen, Geraldine. We really need to talk. I know you probably don't want to hear from me right now, but please, please give me a call."

I went into the bedroom and plopped on the bed.

"Bex, are you having a calamity?" Ray asked as she colored something for school.

"No. I'm fine, Ray."

"Well, you look sad, like you're having a calamity."

I buried my face into the comforter. I needed to finish my homework but it was downstairs with the Queens of Mean and I didn't feel like facing them at that moment. So I did the responsible thing and played pinball on my laptop.

About a half-hour later Aunt Jeanie stuck her head in the door. "Bex, you have a visitor."

I wasn't expecting anyone. "Who is it?"

"That girl," Aunt Jeanie said. Right then I knew it was Geraldine.

"Oh. You can tell her to come up."

"Um, okay." Aunt Jeanie looked like she didn't want Geraldine in her house, like she was going to destroy the place.

"Ray, can I have some privacy please?"

"No way! I'm busy and this is my room too," Ray answered.

"Fine. Stay." I didn't feel like arguing with her.

Moments later Geraldine stood in the doorway wearing a chocolate-chip-cookie-print vest. She was also wearing antennae. "Hello, Earthlings. Fear not. I come in peace."

She was going to make this apology really hard.

Geraldine spotted Ray. "Oh, a tiny Earthling. Can you take me to your leader, little one?"

Ray stared at her wide-eyed. "Uh, I think I'm going to see what Priscilla and Penelope are doing." She ran from the room and shut the door behind her.

"Geraldine, I want—"

"I want my vest back," she said.

"No. You can't give someone something and then take it back."

Geraldine folded her arms across her chest. "I don't make vests for mean people who aren't my friends. Do you know how long I worked on that thing and how much love I put into it?"

"You can't have it back." The truth was she really couldn't have it back. I'd given it to Priscilla and Penelope to play dress up in and they played Fashion Designer with it and cut it up. I swear I had no idea they would destroy it. "Geraldine, please sit down. I want to talk to you."

Geraldine sat on the bed and scowled. "You have fifty-seven seconds to explain yourself."

"Why fifty-seven seconds?" I wondered.

"Fifty-four. Fifty-three."

"Okay, okay." I sat on the bed beside her. "I owe you a huge apology. I shouldn't have said those things I said about you. They were really mean. I guess I just wanted to fit in with someone and I didn't think I could do it if I hung out with you."

"Do I annoy you like I annoy everyone else?" Geraldine asked.

I looked her in the eyes. "Geraldine, I'm going to be honest with you. We don't have a lot in common and I don't understand why you do some of the things you do."

Geraldine nodded. "I know. I'm weird. That's why my mom wants me to be a Silver Rose so bad. So I can fit in somewhere. Hopefully the way the other girls act will rub off on me."

"Trust me, Geraldine. You don't want those awful girls to rub off on you," I assured her.

"I know. But they're so cool and graceful. They say all the right things. They do all the right things. I just want to be normal, but I don't know how to be anyone else but me."

I put my hand on her shoulder. I knew the feeling. "That's just it, Geraldine. You don't need to be anyone other than yourself and you shouldn't try to change just to please someone, not even your mom. Whoever doesn't like you the way you are can keep it moving, and that includes me. I wouldn't blame you if you never wanted to speak to me again."

Geraldine gave me a small smile. "Do you want me to speak to you?"

"Of course. Listen, can we start over?" I asked.

"Sure," Geraldine answered.

I stuck out my hand. "Hi, I'm Bex Carter."

Geraldine shook my hand. "Hi, I'm Geraldine Cordelia Ulysses. Nice to meet you."

"Thanks for forgiving me, Geraldine. I really don't deserve it."

"No problem," she answered. "I'm sorry about what they did to your underwear."

I shrugged. "Typical Ava."

"You should totally get her back. All of them."

"How?" I asked.

Geraldine tapped her finger on her chin. "Give me some time and I'll think of something."

13

Low Friends in High Places

sighs

Junior Silver Rose Candidate Response Journal Page 26
Next session will be your last prep class. How do you
feel about your experience? How do you feel about your
chances of becoming a Junior Silver Rose?

To answer your first question—I'm glad this experience is
over.

Second question—I think there's a fat chance that I will
become a Silver Rose.

The last class took place on Thursday and Aunt Jeanie said it was important for me to look extra nice. I reminded her that she said that for every class and she told me that this was my last chance to earn points and I was seriously behind. I had even stopped keeping track because it was just embarrassing.

I was dreading this class. We had to write an essay about how great we were, practically begging Mrs. Armstrong to let us into the group. The first one I'd written was awful, like all the answers in my response journal. Aunt Jeanie had read my essay, yelled at me, and then written it over herself. I didn't fight with her about it. I knew my chances of making the group were slim, so why bother? I had long given up on my teenage dream room, although I think I deserved it after enduring this torture.

At the meeting we turned in our response journals along with our essays. While the panel read them over and added up our scores, we sat in a room watching a video of the previous year's Coronation ceremony. Let me tell you, it looked like a total snoozefest. Thank goodness I wouldn't have to endure that this year since there was no way I'd be making the group.

The video was almost two hours long and I dozed off in the middle. Each girl had given a brief speech. Then they danced with their escorts and then there was a big dinner.

The lights came back on in the room and Mrs. Armstrong approached the podium. "Ladies, we have tabulated all the scores. Remember you must have at least one hundred points to become a Junior Silver Rose. There were actually two of you who had perfect scores of one-twenty-five. If you have met the minimum score requirement, we will see you at the Coronation ceremony on Sunday where your membership will become official. Please come up when I call your name."

She called the names out in alphabetical order so I was kind of at the top of the list. When Mrs. Armstrong handed me my paper, I quickly folded it over and walked back to my seat. I expected five points, ten at the most, but I didn't want the other girls to see my pitiful score.

In my seat I closed my eyes and then unfolded the paper. I opened one eye and then the other. I blinked a couple of times because I thought my eyes had to be playing tricks on me. According to the paper, I had earned one hundred two points.

My score sheet looked like this:

Attendance: 10 out of 10 points (That one I understood.)

Appearance: 9 out of 10 points (I deserved a 5 at most.)

Social Interaction: 8 out of 10 points (Should've been a 5.)

Business Savvy: 10 out of 10 (Okay. I thought my sports center cupcake thing was a good idea.)

Community Service: 12 out 15 points (???? I didn't even complete a service project!)

Dance: 10 out of 10 (If I deserved that, it was thanks to Austin.)

Response Journal: 13 out of 15 points (Yeah, right!)

Essay: 10 out of 10 points (Maybe, but only because Aunt Jeanie wrote it.)

Beauty Class: 10 out of 10 points

Overall Behavior: 10 out of 10 points (LOL!)

I was stunned. By the other girl's reactions, I could tell that we had all made it. Geraldine had been the only casualty.

"Congratulations, Bex," Amber said after class.

"Thanks, you too," I called over my shoulder. I didn't have time to talk. I had to get to Aunt Jeanie.

"Well?" she asked as I climbed into the passenger seat. She bit her bottom lip nervously.

"I made it," I told her.

She didn't look as surprised as I thought she should. "That's great! Congratulations."

I handed her the paper. "Aunt Jeanie, I shouldn't have made it. I don't deserve all these points."

She started the car as her eyes scanned the paper. "Don't be silly, Bex. You're being too modest."

"I think you need to tell Mrs. Armstrong they made a mistake. Maybe they mixed my scores up with someone else's."

Aunt Jeanie threw the car in reverse and pulled out of the parking spot. "Bex, why on earth would I do that?"

"Because, they gave me twelve points for a community service project that I didn't even complete."

"But you tried. Twice. That counts for something."

115

I looked at my aunt. Why did she want me to be recognized for an honor I didn't earn?

"I get it now," I said. "You did this. You got Mrs. Armstrong to give me more points than I deserved. I should have known. You guys are all friends. I could have done nothing and I still would have made it."

Aunt Jeanie chuckled. "Bex, don't be ridiculous. The Silver Rose Society is a very prestigious and honorable organization. They play strictly by the rules. You made it in fair and square. Why do you have a problem with that?"

I leaned forward so I could get a good look at Aunt Jeanie's neck. It turned red whenever she lied. I didn't know if she even realized that happened. Her neck was a lie detector and at that moment it was as red as a cherry.

I sat back in my seat. She would never tell me the truth. I bet none of the girls had earned all their points. This organization was just a bunch of friends scratching each other's backs. The whole thing was meaningless.

That night Geraldine called me with an idea of how to get back at Ava and the others. I had to talk her out of several of the ideas because I didn't want us to end up in prison. Poisoning the banquet food and making everyone sick was her first idea. Her second was to fake an alien invasion. I told her I planned on doing something more subtle.

***

"Turn around," Aunt Jeanie said inspecting my dress.

I wore a royal blue satin dress that came to my knees. It was spaghetti-strapped with a little jacket over it. It looked nice, but the last thing I wanted to do was spend a night with the phoniest people in the world.

Aunt Alice had come over to watch the kids while Aunt Jeanie, Uncle Bob, and I were at the Coronation ceremony. I was jealous of the others. I would have loved to stay home and hang out with Aunt Alice.

"Bex, you look like a princess. Take pictures for Nana. She'd love to see them," Aunt Alice said, giving me a hug.

"All right, we have to go. We can't be late," Aunt Jeanie said pushing Uncle Bob and me toward the door. We would pick Austin up on the way.

Aunt Jeanie turned around in the car and handed me a stack of index cards. "Here's your speech. Read over it a couple of times."

Each girl had to give a two-minute speech. I had no idea what I planned to say, but it definitely wasn't what was on

those cards. I slid them into the clutch purse Aunt Jeanie
had made me carry. I had a lot of thinking to do.

Austin ran out of his front door as we pulled into the
driveway.

"Tell me he is not wearing sneakers," Aunt Jeanie
muttered under her breath. "Hi, Sandra!" she said waving at
Austin's mom who stood on the porch.

Austin climbed in. He wore black-and-white Converse
sneakers with his three-piece suit. I didn't care what Aunt
Jeanie said. I liked his shoes.

"You look really nice," Austin said.

Aunt Jeanie turned around and stared at both of us.
"What's wrong, Aunt Jeanie?" I asked.

"Nothing," she said, turning around, but she looked like
she wanted to say something else.

When we pulled up to the country club I saw several
girls and women dressed in fabulous gowns and men in
tuxedos entering the building. We left the car with the valet
and went into the ballroom to find our assigned table.

The ceremony started off really boring. A few members
of the Silver Roses gave speeches. After that there was
some kind of candle lighting thing that was supposed to be
symbolic of something, but meant absolutely nothing to
me.

I knew Austin had to be bored out of his mind because he played games on his phone. Aunt Jeanie cleared her throat and glared at him and he put the phone in his jacket pocket. I wondered what fun thing Aunt Alice was doing with the other kids then.

Finally it was time for the part when we became Silver Roses. As our names were called, we were to leave our seats in the audience, walk up front to receive a silver rose pin, and then take a seat on the stage. After that we would give our speeches.

My name was called and I walked up to accept my pin. I prayed that I didn't trip and fall in front of everyone. I still wasn't used to heels.

As I stepped up, Mrs. Armstrong pinned the silver rose she knew very well I didn't deserve to the front of my dress. "Congratulations, Rebecca."

"Thanks," I managed to mutter. I took my seat on the stage and waited until all the other girls had been called.

Then it was time for the speeches. I fiddled with the index cards in my hands. I was nervous about speaking in front of all of these people—especially snobby, superficial people I knew would be judging me.

Summer Anthony was up first. Everyone applauded like crazy for her. I guessed her mother was super popular in this social circle. She waited until the clapping stopped to begin her speech. "First of all I'd like to say thank you to my mother, my family, Mrs. Armstrong, and the panel for making this opportunity possible for me. I am so grateful for this honor and I vow to be a great example for the young women in this community. I will continue to demonstrate good character, selflessness, and compassion."

Was this girl serious? She was the total opposite of all those things.

"When I see someone in need, I will do all I can to help them."

Right. This was the same girl who had treated me and Geraldine like dirt. I blocked out the rest of her phony speech.

Hannah talked about how she would volunteer every weekend at the homeless shelter. I remembered how she would only work fifteen minutes that time we went to the soup kitchen and figured her devoting her weekends to homeless people was a long shot.

Summer and Hannah's speeches were horrible, but Ava's took the cake. "I think one of the biggest problems facing today's youth is bullying. I pledge right now to do all I can to stop bullying in my school."

Well, since she was the bully, that was totally possible.

"In my school I will start an anti-bullying group as well as a support group for victims of bullying."

Really, sign me up since you've bullied me for years! I'm sure the other hundred or so kids that you bully would like to join also.

I was on stage in front of everyone so I tried not to roll my eyes, but I really couldn't help it. This was too much.

What was the point of this organization? These girls were awful and treated people poorly, yet they were applauded and rewarded for it. On top of that, they were total liars.

It was almost my turn. I looked out into the audience at Aunt Jeanie; she was about to dislike me a lot more than she already did. Nothing I did seemed to please her anyway, so I decided to go with my gut.

"Rebecca Lorraine Carter," the emcee announced.

There was applause, but it wasn't for me. It was for Aunt Jeanie. Her friends were clapping for her. They didn't even know me. Shakily, I took my place at the podium. I looked down at the stack of index cards Aunt Jeanie had given me, and then I turned them over so I couldn't see the writing on them. I looked out at all the expectant faces waiting for me to deliver the same sort of phony speech the other girls had.

I took a deep breath. "Good evening, ladies and gentlemen. Before I begin, I should tell you that this is not going to be your usual acceptance speech. This is an unacceptance speech." Was unacceptance a word? I didn't think so. Hey, give me a break; I was making it up as I went along.

There was a bit of a murmur. I didn't even look in Aunt Jeanie's direction. "The purpose of this organization sounds great in theory, but it's all fake. You say you teach character? These girls are some of the most stuck-up, awful people I've ever met. They are the exact opposite of everything you say you stand for, yet you sit here and applaud them." The audience members exchanged surprised glances. I heard gasps coming from behind me. I half expected something to be thrown at the back of my head. "I shouldn't even be standing up here. I didn't earn enough points. But I'm standing here because my aunt is friends with Mrs. Armstrong and the panel—"

I stopped briefly because someone cut the microphone off, but that was okay, I had a big mouth. "So without further ado, I *unaccept* my membership." I removed my Silver Rose pin and threw it onto the floor.

Everyone was in an uproar then. Mrs. Armstrong grabbed the mike from me and pushed me away from the podium.

"I'm so sorry for this, everyone. Let's move right along to our next Silver Rose—"

But then the lights went out in the room. The murmuring stopped and a bright light shone from behind me. Everyone's eyes stared at something on the stage. I turned to see what they were looking at. A video recording from the retreat was projected on the wall. It showed in night vision. Everything was dark, but I could clearly make out the forms of Ava and Summer going through my duffle bag.

"I heard they were huge, like a giant freak," Ava said.

"Well, have you seen her?" Summer said. "They'd have to be."

The person holding the camera turned the camera around, revealing her identity. Geraldine. She gave the camera a wide-eyed look and then pointed it back at Ava and Summer.

"Let's hang them from the banister. She'll be mortified," Ava said.

"It'll serve her right for being a snitch," Ava added.

These were the two girls who had just given speeches about how nice they were and how much they wanted to do for others.

"Who's doing this?" Mrs. Armstrong demanded. "Turn this off immediately!"

The lights came back on. A projector sat in the back of the room, but no one was operating it. Geraldine had come in, did what she had to do, and then left without a trace. Maybe she was some kind of evil genius like Aunt Jeanie.

"We're going to have a brief intermission, then we will continue with our program," Mrs. Armstrong said.

She gently escorted me off the stage. She was being nice, but only because people were watching. "I don't know what you thought you were pulling, young lady, but you've made a very big mistake," she said through clenched teeth.

When we reached our table, Aunt Jeanie and Uncle Bob were already standing.

"Amelia, I am so sorry," Aunt Jeanie said. I'd never seen her look so embarrassed.

"Just get her out of here," Mrs. Armstrong said. "We'll discuss this later."

Half of the ride home was silent except for Uncle Bob's whistling. He apparently wasn't worried about the events that had transpired. Austin had his hand over his mouth trying not to laugh.

I was prepared to stand my ground. I wouldn't apologize for what I'd done and I wouldn't feel bad about it. Then Aunt Jeanie began to cry. Uncle Bob stopped whistling and looked at his wife, but said nothing. Austin and I looked at each other. It was totally awkward.

"Aunt Jeanie, please don't cry," I pleaded. "It's not that serious. I'm sure Penelope and Priscilla will make perfect Silver Roses in a few years."

Aunt Jeanie turned and glared at me. "Are you kidding me? Do you think the Silver Roses will have anything to do with this family after the stunt you pulled?"

"Well, the whole Silver Rose thing is stupid anyway. I mean, what's the point?" I asked.

"The point is," Aunt Jeanie said, "that anyone who's anyone in this town is a Silver Rose."

I didn't think that was a point at all.

"Aunt Jeanie, you should be a leader, not a follower," I told her and then I realized I had gone too far because of the deathly look she gave me. Have you ever seen a scary movie when the killer was about to strike? That was the look. Chills ran up and down my spine.

"How about you just don't talk the rest of the way home? How about that?" Aunt Jeanie asked.

"Fine!" I answered.

"*I said no more talking*!" she screamed. Even Uncle Bob jumped. I knew better than to say anything else so I kept my mouth shut.

When we reached Austin's he gave my hand a little squeeze before he got out. He probably figured that was the last time he would see me.

At home Aunt Jeanie stormed through the house. She even ignored the mess in the living room where Aunt Alice and the kids had been playing some kind of game. That's how I knew she was really mad.

"Back already?" Aunt Alice asked. "What's wrong?"

Aunt Jeanie stopped in the middle of the staircase and took a deep breath. "Maybe Bex should stay with you tonight."

Even though Aunt Jeanie and I had never gotten along, that comment cut me like a knife. Was my aunt actually kicking me out?

"Jeanie, what's going on?" Aunt Alice asked.

"I just need a breather. I think we both need a breather," Aunt Jeanie answered before continuing up the stairs.

Aunt Alice gave me a small smile. "I guess it'll just be you and me, kiddo. We're going to have lots of fun."

Any other time I would have been ecstatic to spend the night with Aunt Alice, but not under these circumstances. If there were any doubt in my mind before, it was gone now. I knew for a fact that Aunt Jeanie hated me.

14

Girl Fight

ducks and hides

"She's on her broom today," Lily-Rose said after school. That was code for "Ava G. is on one of her rampages."

"You really put her in a bad mood, Bex," Chirpy said.

I'd told my friends about what had happened at the Coronation ceremony. They were very proud of me, but they were also fearful of my safety, and thereby fearful of their safety, you know, being guilty by association and everything. I had been successful in avoiding Ava G. all day until lunch time when she had bumped into me and spilled iced tea in my lap "by accident."

"Did you guys hear?" Santiago asked, coming up behind me. "Kristen challenged Ava to a fight tomorrow after school."

"Are you serious?" I asked. "What's that supposed to prove?"

Santiago shrugged. "I guess the winner will be the real Queen Bee of the seventh grade. My money's on Kristen. I think she's going to mop the floor with Ava and Ava deserves it. I'm taking bets if you're interested."

We called Santiago the Hustler. Every week he came up with a new way of making money. So far he'd run a bodyguard service for kids to buy bully protection, he sold real genuine hall passes, and he'd run a matchmaking service for last year's Valentine Dance. Those were just a few of his business endeavors. I imagined that Santiago had to be filthy rich by now.

I had mixed feelings about this fight. I couldn't stand Ava, but I didn't want the girl to get beaten up. However, it wasn't my business, so I was staying out of it.

Since I had spent the night at Aunt Alice's, this would be the first time I would see Aunt Jeanie since our fight.

When I got home I heard two voices talking in the dining room. I heard the words "teenager," "moody," and "I give up." I knew Aunt Jeanie was talking to our social worker, Ms. Larson. I headed upstairs. I didn't think I wanted to hear how Aunt Jeanie really felt about me. I went to my room to do my homework and stay under the radar.

Later that evening Mrs. Groves came over with Ava. Aunt Jeanie called me downstairs. Mrs. Groves stood in the entryway looking very uncomfortable. "Why don't you girls go upstairs?" she said to Ava and me.

Ava for once didn't look like she'd rather be dead than spend time with me. As we walked up the stairs, I heard Mrs. Groves say something quietly to my aunt. "It's nothing personal. I just don't want her to take Ava down with her."

Mrs. Groves didn't want her daughter to hang out with me anymore because of what had happened with the Silver Roses. That was fine with me. Neither one of us had wanted this phony friendship to begin with.

Ava closed the door to Ray's and my room. "I really, really need your help, Bex."

That was a first. "You need my help with what?" I asked suspiciously. I almost reminded her that she had spilled a beverage on my lap only hours ago.

"I need you to help me fight Kristen tomorrow."

"No way! I'm not going to fight anyone. You got yourself involved in this stupid girl fight, so now you can deal with it."

Ava put on this sad little puppy dog face that was absolutely not going to work on me. "Please, Bex. Normally I wouldn't be afraid, but Kristen has a black belt in karate. She's going to clobber me and then everyone's going to treat me like a complete loser."

I sat at my desk and opened my laptop. "Yeah, maybe you should experience that feeling sometime and then you wouldn't be so mean."

"Beeex," she whined. "Look, you don't really have to fight her, just act like you're going to. When she sees you, she'll run in the other direction."

"Why would that be, Ava? I'm not exactly intimidating," I pointed out.

"Because you're huge, that's why!"

What was I, a Godzilla-Sumo-Wrestling-Amazon-Woman?

"Nope, sorry," I told her.

"You have to. It's the least you could do for humiliating me at the Silver Rose ceremony. Bex, I was traumatized after that."

I stood and looked her in the eye. "You were traumatized? How do you think I felt when you hung my underwear up for everyone to see and then took a picture of it?"

"Yes, but I didn't text the picture to everyone like I said I would. That should count for something," she said.

I stepped closer to her. "It doesn't."

"Oh, yeah?" She pulled her phone from her purse. "I tried to be nice to you, Bex. How about I send that picture to everyone right now?"

I stepped even closer to her. Our noses were almost touching. "Go ahead. Do it," I said, calling her bluff. I knew how Ava's twisted little mind worked. The reason she hadn't texted the picture to everyone had nothing to do with her being nice to me. Not too long ago, we'd had an assembly on cyber-bullying and she knew how much trouble she could get in for sharing something like that.

I narrowed my eyes at her so she would know I meant business. "Ava, I know you're not used to hearing no, but no. I'm sorry. If I were you I would just squash this stupid thing with Kristen."

She folded her arms across her chest. "Bex Carter, you are totally useless!"

"Yeah, yeah, yeah. If I were you I'd be YouTubing some karate moves. Good luck."

Ava stormed out of the room, slamming the door behind her. What did she expect from me? She'd dug herself into this hole and then expected me to do her dirty work for her when she'd always been so mean to me.

The following day as I was leaving school, I saw a crowd forming in the field on the side of the school. My heart dropped. I couldn't believe they were actually going through with this foolishness.

"Let's go!" Marishca said. "Not zat I condone violence, but I want to see what's going to happen."

"Come on, Bex," Chirpy said. "This may be your once-in-a-lifetime opportunity to see Ava the Terrible get put in her place."

Lily-Rose grabbed my arm and pulled me toward the field. "Come on. It's going to happen whether we watch or not, so we might as well watch, right?"

I heard the chanting as we neared the crowd. "Fight! Fight! Fight! Fight!"

I pushed my way through the kids to see what was happening. Ava and Kristen stood facing each other. Ava looked terrified and Kristen looked like she wanted to eat Ava for dinner. Ava didn't stand a chance.

Then something strange happened. Kristen's hungry gaze fell on me. "Oh, there she is. Let's go, Bex."

Everyone stared at me. "Huh? What are you talking about?"

"Ava said you were going to take her place and fight me. I didn't know you were her bodyguard."

Ava pushed me forward and stood behind me. "Please, Bex. Think of all the wonderful times we've had together."

I couldn't think of one wonderful time we've shared. I definitely wasn't about to fight about something that had absolutely nothing to do with me. Kristen seemed like she could be a reasonable person so I decided to take the opportunity to get her to understand how stupid fighting was.

"Listen, Kristen," I said. "I know you and Ava have your problems but this isn't the way to solve them. Use your words. Why don't you tell Ava what your problem is with her?"

Kristen bent her knees and held her hands up. "No more talking. Let's go."

"Okay," I said looking behind me. "Maybe Ava would like to start the conversation. Ava, why don't you tell Kristen what your problem is with her?"

Ava's green eyes grew wide. "Bex!"

Before I could turn around to see what she was looking at, I felt a kick to my back. A sharp pain shot up and down my spine.

"Ooohhhh," went the crowd.

"No, you did not just do that! You are cruisin' for a bruisin'!" Chirpy yelled. She ran toward Kristen and did some kind of spinning kick thing, but Kristen backed up and Chirpy missed her entirely. Marishca grabbed Kristen's leg and pulled it. Kristen fell to the ground. Lily-Rose jumped in. Before I knew it there was a full-out brawl going on.

"Break it up! Break it up!" yelled Mr. Benson, one of the science teachers.

After I stood and brushed the grass from my knees, I saw him holding Lily-Rose with one arm and Marishca with the other. Kristen had Chirpy in a headlock and Ava was nowhere to be found.

"All of you girls, get to the principal's office now!" Mr. Benson bellowed.

The five of us sat in Principal Radcliff's office, trying to explain ourselves at the same time.

"Kristen started it," I said.

"She kicked my friend," Chirpy said.

"It was self-defense," Lily-Rose said.

"I was just trying to break it up," Marishca explained.

"The four of them attacked me," Kristen lied.

Principal Radcliff banged on his desk. "Hey, hey, hey. One at a time. Bex, you were the one on the ground. Tell me what happened."

"This isn't their fault. Kristen wanted to fight Ava G. I was trying to stop it and Kristen karate kicked me in the back. My friends were only trying to defend me. Wouldn't you do the same if someone had hurt your friend?"

Kristen kept insisting that we had attacked her, but Principal Radcliff said he would look at the security cameras to see who was telling the truth. Until then we were all suspended until further notice.

I felt bad for my friends who had only been trying to defend me. I knew Lily-Rose's parents would flip. They'd blown a gasket when Lily-Rose had gotten her first detention because of me.

"I'm so sorry, guys," I said as we sat in the front office while the principal called our parents.

"It wasn't your fault," Chirpy said.

"Thanks for having my back," I said. I would have definitely lost in a fight against Kristen.

"Of course," said Lily-Rose. "If someone wants to fight one of us, they have to go through all of us."

See why I love these girls?

15

Truce

—feeling hopeful ☺

"I give up. I just don't know what to do with her anymore. Now she's fighting at school," Aunt Jeanie complained to Ms. Larson.

I had explained to her exactly what happened and how it really wasn't my fault, but she didn't want to hear it.

Ms. Larson had been taking notes on a notepad. She sighed and put the cap on her pen. I imagined she was sick of dealing with us. "Why don't Bex and I go somewhere and have a talk? Just the two of us."

Aunt Jeanie threw her hands up. "Fine."

Ms. Larson took me to a coffee shop, but neither of us ordered anything. I wasn't hungry or thirsty. All I wanted was to go back and live at Nana's. It was obvious that Aunt Jeanie and I would never ever get along.

"I see what you're talking about, Bex," Ms. Larson said. "Your aunt is something else. I'd hate to have to live with her."

I shrugged.

"I mean she seems like she's just evil, like the wicked stepmother in *Cinderella.*"

"She's not as bad as that," I muttered.

"I think she might be worse. She's mean and stuck-up and overbearing and—"

"Hey!" I shouted. "You can't talk about my aunt like that!"

Ms. Larson frowned. "Why not? You do."

"I know, but that's different, it—"

"Aww, come on, Bex. She's awful. Admit it."

"No, she's not. She took me and my sister in and she buys me nice clothes and gave me a wonderful thirteenth birthday party. She makes sure that we eat well and pays for Reagan to go to a private school and to take ballet lessons and she—" I stopped talking when I realized what she had done. Well-played, Ms. Larson, well-played.

"I guess you get my point. Bex, look at me."

I looked her in the eye.

"I know living with your aunt may not be a walk in the park, but I truly think she's doing the best she can. She may not be perfect, but nobody is."

"Yes, but she's so mean to me," I said.

"Listen, trust me. I know your aunt can be a handful, but put yourself in her shoes. Think about how she feels. It's not easy to take two extra children under your wing. Reagan can be a handful and it's never easy raising a teenager. Think about your Nana—that's your Aunt Jeanie's mother. It's not easy for her to watch her mom deteriorate like that. And your mother—that's her sister. Imagine how worried she must be about her. She may not do everything right, but she's allowed to be human, Bex."

I began to cry because Ms. Larson was absolutely right. I was so absorbed in my own problems; I never realized that some of them were Aunt Jeanie's problems, too.

Ms. Larson took my hand. "Bex, I know this situation isn't perfect and you and your aunt may clash at times, but she really is doing the best she can. I don't think she's going out of her way to hurt you. Try to meet her halfway."

I told Ms. Larson that I would try, but Aunt Jeanie didn't make it very easy.

* * *

"How many days are you guys suspended for?" I asked Lily-Rose on the phone that evening.

"Three. I'm grounded indefinitely."

"I'm so sorry." Principal Radcliff had viewed the video tape. Everyone involved had gotten suspended except for me because I hadn't hit anyone. I felt so bad that my friends would now have a suspension on their records when they had only been trying to defend me. I would take all their suspensions if I could. Sure, a couple weeks off from school would be torture—but I'd do it for my friends.

I heard Lily-Rose's mom yell something in the background. "I have to go. I'll see you in a few days, I guess."

"Okay. Bye, Lily-Rose." I hung up the phone. It was time for me to have a conversation I'd been dreading, but it needed to be done.

I knocked on Aunt Jeanie's bedroom door.

"You're not sleeping in here tonight, Francois," Aunt Jeanie called.

"It's Bex."

"Oh. Come in."

Aunt Jeanie was rubbing lotion on her hands preparing for bed. I could hear Uncle Bob singing in the shower.

"Can I talk to you for a minute?" I asked.

"Sure. Sit." Aunt Jeanie and I both took a seat on the bench in front of her vanity. "What's up?"

I thought about how I should say this. I didn't want this discussion to turn into another argument. "Remember the other day when I told you and Mrs. Groves that you shouldn't talk about people behind their backs?"

"Yes."

"Well, I should take my own advice."

Aunt Jeanie looked puzzled. "Meaning?"

Just come out and say it, Bex. "Sometimes behind your back I call you Aunt Meanie."

Aunt Jeanie looked away from me. I could tell she was hurt. Maybe I shouldn't have told her. "Oh. I guess I deserve that sometimes."

"No, you don't. You do so much for me and Ray and I really appreciate it. I'll never ever call you that again."

"Okay," Aunt Jeanie said. "And I'll try to be less of a meanie. Maybe I wanted you to become a Silver Rose for me instead of for you, and that was wrong. And you were right about what you told me and Mrs. Groves the other day."

"I was?" I didn't think I'd ever hear Aunt Jeanie utter the words, "You were right."

141

She took a deep breath. "Yes, we shouldn't talk poorly about people behind their backs. I wouldn't want my friends doing that to me and it doesn't set a good example for you all. Thank you for teaching me that."

I nodded. I hoped she and Mrs. Groves would stop their gossiping. "I don't want to fight with you all the time, but I need you to understand that I can't be anybody but me. I'm not Silver Rose material and I'll never be anything like Ava."

Aunt Jeanie smiled. "Okay. I'll try to remember that. And if I overstep my boundaries, just give me a little reminder."

"Will you listen?"

She put her hand on my cheek. "I will, Bex. Regardless of what you may think, I love you."

"I love you, too, Aunt Jeanie. I'm sorry I'm such a pain sometimes."

"I'm sorry I'm so hard on you sometimes. I just want you to be the best person you can be." She pulled me close to her and I let her. I hoped we would keep the promises we'd made to one another. I went back to the mental scoreboard in my head:

~~Bex: 2   Aunt Jeanie: 4~~

It's a draw.

16

New Friends

smiles

Aunt Alice invited me to spend the weekend with her, just the two of us. Surprisingly, Aunt Jeanie didn't object.

"Be good," was all she said as Aunt Alice and I left the house. I was shocked not to get her usual list warning me of what I wasn't supposed to eat, watch, or do. Maybe she really was trying.

We spent the weekend watching old black-and-white movies. I usually thought they were boring, but somehow watching them with Aunt Alice made them fun. She showed me the pictures she had taken on her latest trip to Japan and we had girl talk. I even told her about my conversation with Aunt Jeanie.

"That was very mature of you, Bex," Aunt Alice said. "I'm proud of you."

The weekend had been so much fun, I almost didn't want to go back home Sunday night.

I went into the bedroom and tossed my duffle bag on the bed. Ray was doing a puzzle on the floor. "Hey, get out of my room!"

"This is our room, Ray. Nice to see you too."

"This is not our room. It's all mine, now get out!"

I ignored her and went to grab my laptop from the desk, but it wasn't there. I noticed that all my stuff was gone from the desk and from the dressers.

"Uh, Ray. Where's my stuff?"

She pressed another puzzle piece into place. "Where it's supposed to be," she answered.

"No, it's not. I don't see it."

"Well, why would it be in here, silly? I told you this isn't your room. Your room is down the hall now, the last door on the left."

It took a few seconds for me to realize what she meant. It couldn't be. That meant that after almost a year, Aunt Jeanie had broken down and was letting me move into the open guestroom.

I ran down the hallway to the last room on the left and threw the door open. I screamed. There it was, my dream room. The one Aunt Jeanie had shown me pictures of. Moments later, everyone gathered in the doorway.

"Do you like it?" Aunt Jeanie asked.

"Like it? I love it!" I felt like I was dreaming as I looked around the room. The walls were a nice shade of gray except for one that was bright yellow. The gray walls had green and yellow designs painted on them. One wall had a cupcake, the other had a soccer ball, and the other had my name painted on it. "Aunt Jeanie, Uncle Bob, I don't know what to say."

I walked around the room and ran my hands over the white furniture. I climbed the stairs to my cool new bed. Priscilla, Penelope, Francois, and Ray ran around my room buzzing with excitement.

"Don't get used to this, guys," I warned them. "None of you can be in here without my permission."

"Aww," Ray whined, "not even me?"

"Especially not you," I said. I couldn't wait to tell my friends about my brand new room. Of the four of us, I'd been the only one who didn't have my own room until now. My eyes welled with tears—happy tears. I gave Aunt Jeanie and Uncle Bob a hug. "I know I didn't earn this, Aunt Jeanie. I didn't become a Silver Rose."

"I know, but you did try, kind of, and I agree with you that you should have your own space. Of course I expect you to keep your room clean and keep up with your chores."

"I will, I will, I will! I promise!"

My family left me alone to enjoy my new space. I plopped on my bed and stared at the ceiling. Taking in a deep breath, I exhaled. Finally, something in my life had gone right.

That Friday was Chirpy's turn to host the sleepover, but I insisted on moving it to Aunt Jeanie's so we could enjoy my new room. Lily-Rose couldn't come since she was grounded forever, so I invited Geraldine. She was strange, but I hoped she would grow on the other girls like she had grown on me.

The four of us gathered in front of my new bedroom. Turning the doorknob, I pushed the door open. "Ta-da!" The girls gasped.

"Bex, this room is amazing," Chirpy said.

"Do you need a roommate?" Marishca asked.

"The feng shui in here is amazing. I like that it's rectangular rather than square. That makes a difference, you know." (You can guess who said that.)

Geraldine unzipped her duffle bag. "I have a big surprise for you guys!"

Surprises from Geraldine generally weren't a good thing.

She reached into her bag and pulled something out. "Ta-daaaaa!" Geraldine pulled out four vests. "Chirpy, this one is for you," she said handing Chirpy a vest covered with little people swimming. "Since you're a swimmer."

Chirpy took the vest and examined it. "Wow. Isn't this-"

I shot her a look.

"Special," she finished. "Thanks, Geraldine."

Geraldine handed Marishca a vest with girls doing handstands. "Since you're a gymnast."

"Oh, yeah. I should totally rock this at my next competizhun." Marishca looked at me from the corner of her eye. I gave her a thumbs-up.

Don't ask me how Geraldine knew Chirpy was a swimmer and Marishca did gymnastics. I figured it was best not to know.

Geraldine held up the next vest, a white one covered with black musical notes. "This one is for Lily-Rose. We can give it to her when she's not grounded anymore."

I laughed at my friends. "You guys are going to look really nifty in those sporty vests. Why don't you try them on?"

Chirpy and Marishca glared at me. If looks could kill . . . But they tried the vests on and they fit perfectly.

"Who's the last one for?" Chirpy asked.

"This one is for Bex!" Geraldine announced.

"B-but you already gave me a vest, remember?"

Geraldine handed me the balled-up vest. "Sure, but you can never have too many vests."

I held it up. This one wasn't covered in soccer balls like the other one; it was covered in hearts.

"I made you that because you have a lot of heart. It took a lot of guts to do what you did at the Silver Rose ceremony."

"Aww, thanks so much, Geraldine," I said as I slid on my vest. "I love it." I wouldn't be giving away this one to my little cousins.

"Listen, guys," Geraldine said. "I know vests aren't in style right now so I don't want you to feel obligated to wear them or anything—"

"Are you kidding me?" I asked. "Who cares about what's in style? We're going to rock these at the mall tomorrow."

Geraldine's face brightened. "Really?"

"Really?" Marishca asked. She and Chirpy looked at me as if I'd lost my mind. Maybe I had gone a little too far, but I was sure I could talk them into it.

"Sure, why not?" Chirpy replied through gritted teeth.

"Yay!" Geraldine said, clapping. "Now we're *vest* friends!"

Oh boy.

The four of us stretched out on the furry rug that lay in the middle of the room.

"What should we do tonight?" Chirpy asked.

"We should do something fun," I answered. "No makeovers!"

"Let's prank call Lily-Rose and pretend that we're an ax murderer looking zrough her window!" Marishca suggested.

"No," Chirpy said. "We'll tell her we're calling from her closet. It'll be a gas!"

These were the fun-loving girls that I knew. "I love it, but she has caller ID," I reminded them.

Geraldine grinned. "That won't stop me. I have caller ID blocking. Sometimes I have to make anonymous calls to NASA when I spot suspicious flying objects."

Chirpy patted Geraldine on the back. "This may be the beginning of a beautiful friendship."

Geraldine brought me her phone and I dialed Lily-Rose's number. "I'm putting it on speaker. No laughing."

"Hello?" she whispered, probably because she wasn't supposed to be on the phone.

"Hello, Lily-Rose," I said in my deepest, creepiest voice.

"Maverick?"

"Who's Maverick?" I asked.

"Who is this?" She sounded nervous.

"This is the man who's hiding in your closet with an ax!"

"Wh-what?" she stammered. I knew she was really scared.

"Yes, why don't you come check?"

"Okay, I will," she said, sounding suddenly brave. I wasn't expecting that. I heard her closet door sliding open. "Let's see," she said. "I'm rummaging through my clothes and I don't see any—wait, there's a man's black shoe and a shiny metal—" She screamed and made a gurgling sound.

The four of us backed away from the phone.

"Lily-Rose?" Chirpy yelled. "Are you okay?"

I heard things moving and bumping in the background and then there was finally silence.

"L-Lily-Rose?" Marishca said, in a tiny voice.

"Seriously, you guys really thought I was going to fall for that?" Lily-Rose asked.

I breathed a sigh of relief that my friend was still alive and the five of us laughed hysterically. That was until we heard Mr. Johnston's voice.

"Lily-Rose, give me that phone!" he yelled.

"But, but, but," Lily-Rose said and then the line went dead.

We fell into giggles again and then decided to call Ava next. I looked around at my friends, both old and new. I had a beautiful new bedroom, great friends who stuck up for me, and a family who loved me. Life was good.

Bex: Infinity!

Life lesson from Bex: Be a real friend. Being a fake friend is totally lame.

Keep Reading for a preview of All's Fair In Love and War (The Bex Carter Series)
Available Winter 2013

I glared at Ava and she narrowed her eyes at me. We both knew she needed math tutoring like she needed another hole in the head.

"Yes," Mrs. Groves said. "I don't know what happened. Ava's always done great in math and all of a sudden last week she started having a hard time. We want to get her help now before she falls behind. My Ava has never gotten anything less than an A."

I couldn't believe her. She didn't take her gaze off me even as she opened her math book to the chapter we were on.

"Carter, like always, help yourself to anything in the fridge," Aunt Jeanie said.

"Ava, I'll be back to pick you up after we're done at the club," Mrs. Groves announced as she and Aunt Jeanie left chatting away.

"I'll be in the kitchen getting dinner started," Aunt Alice told us. "Let me know if you need anything."

"Okay, Aunt Alice," I replied still staring at Ava.

"All right," Carter said. "Let's start on page 118, problem number one."

Ava and I both found the page and Carter began to explain. He sat at the head of the table with Ava and I on either side of him. As he spoke I noticed Ava inching her chair closer and closer to him. I needed to concentrate and she was totally distracting me. Ava had an advantage, she really didn't need to pay attention to Carter's explanations, but I did.

I couldn't let her get closer to Carter than I was. Every time she moved her chair over an inch, I moved mine over two inches. Pretty soon we'd both be sitting on his lap.

"What are you guys doing?" Carter asked once we were so close, we couldn't get any closer.

"Uh, I wanted to move closer so I can hear you better," I said.

"I moved closer because I like the way you smell," Ava said boldly.

My jaw almost hit the table. I couldn't believe she was being so flirtatious and straight forward with him. Who does that?

Carter cleared his throat. "I'm going to go into the kitchen and get a drink of water."

"I'll get it for you," I offered.

"No, that's all right. I'll get it," he insisted.

"I can't believe you," I told Ava once Carter was out of the room. "You're failing math on purpose just to get tutored by a cute boy. Do you have any idea how pathetic that is?"

"What's pathetic is you thinking a boy like Carter would be interested in you. I see the way you drool over him."

I was about to say something back, but Carter returned.

"Okay, where were we?" he asked after taking a swig from the water bottle.

The rest of the lesson was a blur. It was hard enough for me to focus with Carter teaching me, but now with Ava sitting across from me shooting me dirty looks it was nearly impossible. How was I supposed to bring my math grade up now?

Join the mailing list to be notified of new releases:
http://eepurl.com/HappH

Other Books by Tiffany Nicole Smith
The Fairylicious Series (Books 1-6)
The Bex Carter Series:
All's Fair In Love and Math (Winter 2013)
Winter Blunderland (Winter 2013)
Camp Lie-A-Lot (Winter 2013)
The Great War of Lincoln Middle (January 2014)

authortiffanynicole.com

Made in the USA
Middletown, DE
01 May 2017